AWAY FROM KEYBOARD

SAVING THEIR FOREVER

PATRICIA D. EDDY

If you love steamy romantic suspense, I'd love to send you an exclusive short story set in Dublin, Ireland. Castles & Kings is ONLY available for my newsletter subscribers. Visit my website and let me know where to send your free short story! http://patriciadeddy.com

CHAPTER ONE

Wren

"Stop. I can stand up on my own." I glare at Ryker, then brace my hand on the back of the couch for leverage. With only ten days until I'm officially *overdue*, simple things like getting up from the sofa aren't so easy anymore.

"Prove it," he mutters. Then almost immediately shakes his head. "Never mind. Don't." Before I can stop him, he snags me under the arms and gently lifts me to my feet. "Are you sure you don't want me to stay?"

I roll my eyes. "You're bouncing off the walls, Ry. No missions, only one training session a week..." I link my small, swollen fingers with his thick, massive ones, and squeeze gently. "I know you think you can walk away from it all, but that's never going to happen, soldier. Hidden Agenda is your home. Your family. You can't go on every mission anymore. But you can't ignore them either."

Ryker sobers, wrapping his arms around me and pulling me close. "I don't know how to do this, little bird. Be there for you and the baby, but still save people. Because if I can't..."

"You won't be Ryker McCabe. The man I fell in love with. The man who saved me." I tip my head back to peer up at him. "You can do both, Ry. Maybe not for the first month, but after that... You think I'll suddenly ignore my computers the moment the doctor puts the baby in my arms? Horsepucky. I'll work *less*, but hacking is who I am. What I do. Hidden Agenda and Second Sight need me, and I need them too. Plus, how else am I going to teach our daughter the importance of tech skills?"

He chuckles, then bends down to press a kiss to my belly. The baby chooses that exact moment to punch—or kick— hard enough she hits Ry in the nose.

His eyes widen, and he rubs his hand over the green fleece sweatshirt with "Loading..." emblazoned across the front. "She's going to be a fighter."

"Or she just *really* wants out." I rub my lower back. "If the doctor called and offered to induce me tomorrow, I would be so there for it."

"Ten days, little bird." He wraps his arms around me from behind, cradling my belly in such a way, I feel safe and protected. And loved. Always loved. This giant of a man can be so tender—almost delicate—with me. When we first met, it was hard to imagine he could be anything but big and loud and brutish. He's none of those things, though. The hard, gruff exterior is who he thinks he has to be. But it's not who he is. Not at all.

I rest my head against his chest. "Don't you mean Big Bird? I'm the size of your truck. Or...you."

"You are not—"

"I can't see my toes. I can't put on my own socks or tie my shoes. And the peeing. Spitsnacks. I have to go. Again."

I waddle off toward the bathroom. You'd think somewhere along the evolutionary journey, someone would have thought, "Oh, once the baby's born, the mother isn't going to sleep for six months or more. So maybe...let's let her sleep up *until* birth." No. I'm up every hour *just* to pee. And then again whenever baby girl decides she wants to go dancing.

A cramp steals my breath as I dry my hands. They've been happening more and more the past week. Normal—according to my doctor—but the first one was terrifying. Thank goodness Ryker wasn't home that day. The man didn't flinch when we were being chased by armed thugs in Russia, but if I so much as wince, he's ready to break every traffic law in the world to get me to the hospital in record time.

"You're pale," he says when I return to the kitchen to make a cup of tea. "What's wrong?"

Ignoring him, I offer a dismissive wave of my hand as I brush by, hoping he won't press the issue. I should know better by now.

"Wren." He takes me by the shoulders, turning me toward him. "What's. Wrong?"

Reaching up, I trail my fingers along his jaw. "Nothing, Ry. Just a cramp. Situation Normal."

The look in his eyes is anything but *normal*. "I'm canceling training. And calling off the shower."

"No, you're not." I take a step back and glare up at him. "Braxton Hicks contractions are totally normal. They don't mean anything. They're my body getting ready for labor. But they can happen for *weeks* before birth."

"How long has this been going on?" he growls. I see so much emotion in his eyes. Fear. Concern. Love.

"Stand down, soldier. Dr. Robin said there's nothing to worry about unless my water breaks or I start bleeding."

"You're my entire world, Wren," Ry says, his voice rougher than I've heard it in months. "If anything happens to you..."

"The only thing that's going to happen to me this afternoon is that I'm going to eat so much cake that I fall asleep in the recliner the moment everyone leaves."

"I should still stay."

I laugh at the idea of my bald, scarred, mountain of a husband standing guard over me at my flippin' baby shower. "You want to spend the afternoon with a bunch of women talking about childbirth and breastfeeding and periods? You wouldn't last an hour."

"Little bird, I spent fifteen months in Hell. I think I can handle a single afternoon with seven women."

As if the Universe is out to prove him wrong, the doorbell rings at that exact moment. Ryker presses his palm to the scanner to unlock the door and gapes.

Cara thrusts a pan of lasagna at him, then darts back down the hall to the elevator. "I've got another huge casserole downstairs. Put that one in the oven at three-fifty!"

"Sorry," Hope says as she squeezes past Ry. "The doctor doesn't want me carrying anything heavier than three pounds, and Wyatt has his hands full."

"Where do you want...all of this?" Wyatt asks. A diaper bag is slung over his shoulder—the nicest one on the market—and his other arm is buried under a stack of blankets, and a body pillow. When Ry just blinks at him, he strolls by, shaking his head.

Hope passes me a small, pink bag that smells like heaven—and my favorite body lotion.

"Crap on a cracker. I thought we agreed 'only baby clothes and spit-up cloths'?" I didn't want a big, fussy shower. Just my closest friends together for a silly afternoon with no responsibilities before my life changes forever.

"Like we were going to listen. Harlow is going to be the most pampered little girl in all of Seattle." Hope beams as she leans gingerly against the counter.

Carefully, I step forward and wrap an arm around her. The back brace is bulky under her light blue sweater. "How much longer do you have to be in this contraption?"

She sighs. "Another three weeks. At least I don't need the cervical collar anymore. I felt like I was choking the whole time."

After her ex had her dragged down a flight of concrete stairs a few months ago, Hope broke two vertebrae. It's only in the past two weeks that she's been able to walk without pain.

"Sit down. You look exhausted." I slip my arm through hers and try to lead her to the couch, but she shakes her head.

"Don't take this the wrong way, Wren, but your furniture is all too comfortable. It's easier if I sit up straight—or just stand. Otherwise, all this plastic digs into my hips, and it's torture."

Ry disappears into the back room while Wyatt piles gift after gift in the corner by the bassinet. When he's done, he moves to Hope's side and rubs his big hands up and down her arms. "If you need me to come home early, call."

"Our place is only two floors down, stud," she says with a laugh. "I think I can make it there myself."

"And if not," Cara calls, breezing back into the condo with a second tray of lasagna, "I'll get her home. We've got this, boys. Go save the world. Or train to, anyway."

Ry drags a solid, wooden chair into the living room. "Will this do, Hope?"

"It's perfect," she says, easing herself down onto the hard seat and sighing. "I swear all physical therapists are sadists. I've never done so many squats, leg raises, and glute bridges in my life. Every muscle in my body aches. All the time."

"When I get home tonight, darlin'," Wyatt says with a wink, "we'll see how sore you are."

Her cheeks flush a dark red.

"That's it," I say, pointing to the door. "The pregnant lady is putting her foot down. Ry? Wyatt? Time to go."

Ryker wraps his arms around me, cups the back of my neck, and angles my head so he can claim my lips. The kiss leaves me breathless—and wet. I shouldn't want him this badly. Not when I'm as big as a house. But I do. The books say the last few weeks of pregnancy can leave a woman incredibly...needy, but I didn't think it would be *this* bad.

My nipples pebble against my bra, and I dig my fingers into Ry's biceps. If we had time—and privacy—I'd drag him back to our bedroom and tear his clothes off. But at that moment, someone whistles behind me.

I break off the kiss, and shove at Ry's chest. "Go. Now."

My knees sway for a beat when he releases me. "Call me if you need *anything*."

"I know, I know."

The door shuts behind Ry and Wyatt before I notice Inara and Raelynn standing in the kitchen, looking anywhere but at me.

"You weren't much better," I say, grinning at Inara when she meets my gaze. "I seem to remember you making some pretty big puppy dog eyes in Russia when you found out you could call Royce."

She turns and starts rummaging in the fridge. "You want a beer, probie?"

"Uh..." Raelynn, the newest member of Hidden Agenda darts a quick gaze to me, then looks back down at the floor. She's still struggling to accept this new family of hers. Of ours. "Wyatt's trainin' with the guys today. There some reason you're still callin' me 'probie'?"

"Because I can?" Inara passes her a bottle of Pilsner, and I stare longingly at the local brew. Of everything I've had to give up the past nine months, beer is what I miss the most. Even more than the truly epic amount of coffee I used to drink. My single cup a day now barely cuts it, and sparkling water only gets me so far.

Raelynn's shoulders dip when she sees the longing written all over my face. "Sorry, Wren. I can have somethin' else. *We* can have somethin' else." She elbows Inara in the ribs, and the sniper's gray eyes meet mine.

"Oh, shit. I didn't think—"

"It's fine." I shrug, forcing a smile. "This is a party. I'm only *a little* jealous. Besides, I've already told Ry he has one job after the baby's born. In under twelve hours, he needs to bring me an ice cold beer."

"Oh, please." Inara shakes her head. "Like he's going to leave your side or let Harlow out of his sight for the next, oh... eighteen years? We'll never see him again. West will take over Hidden Agenda, and Ry will be nothing more than a memory."

"He won't be *that* bad." I take my decaf iced tea and shuffle into the living room to sink down onto the couch. And then it hits me. "Oh, spitsnacks. He'll be worse, won't he? Hiring a dozen bodyguards to watch over us whenever we leave the building, buying a fudging preschool rather than letting her go off somewhere he can't completely control..."

"The man, the myth, the legend. Ryker McCabe," Inara says with a chuckle. "New recruits will hear stories about a mysterious giant, angry man who loved one-word answers and barking out orders. There will be whispers. Rumors. But only us old-timers will have ever met the man."

Raelynn chokes on a sip of her beer. "Well, shee-it," she manages, wiping her nose on her sleeve. "Am I supposed to be an 'old-timer'?" After a beat, she swears. "Fuck. I'm two years older than you. Wren, I'm gonna need somethin' stronger than beer."

I love these women. Cara, Hope, Inara...even Raelynn, though I wouldn't consider us "friends" yet. When the whole team—family—gets together, I fit in. We all do. But despite that, I've never been very good at "girl talk." Even this baby shower had conditions. I made Inara promise there wouldn't be any games. No "sniff the baby food" or "diaper a balloon." And God help anyone who tries to measure my belly with toilet paper.

Cara pops the top on a bottle of sparkling cider as Evianna's voice carries over the intercom. "We're here! We're finally here!"

Inara uses her code to let Evianna and Cam in. Ry's so overprotective, the door *never* stays unlocked for more than a few seconds. "Sorry," Evianna calls as she breezes into the condo, laden down with half a dozen gift bags. "The car service got lost on the way to the hotel, then couldn't find Cam's house for a full fifteen minutes. I was on the phone with Dax when the driver *finally* figured it out."

Cam sinks onto the loveseat with a sigh. Pixel immediately prances over and drops a squeaky toy into her lap. "All right, puffball," she says and tosses the fuzzy donut across the room. "But only because you're so polite."

I don't get up to hug either of the women. Evianna's heard all about my swollen ankles, lack of sleep, backaches, and carpal tunnel. She wraps her arm around me and presses a kiss to the top of my head. "How you doing, hon?"

Better now.

"I'm glad you're here," I whisper. "You're staying, right? Until...?"

"Until you and Ryker tell us to go back to Boston. Or at least two weeks."

The relief is so intense, I shiver.

Evianna, Cam, and I speak the same language. Awkward geek. Zephyr too, but she's on a case for Austin and working fifteen-hour days. So having them—along with Cara, who keeps me in lasagna and secretly binges reality TV with me whenever the guys go to Hidden Agenda—here with me now is more of a comfort than I realized.

These last few weeks, whenever Harlow moves, I wonder if she knows that soon, everything is going to change. That she's going to be in this big, scary world with sights and sounds and cars and *dogs*. That she'll have to eat and be bathed and changed. She'll be hot and cold and hungry and sleepy and happy and sad...and her parents won't always know what's wrong. Let alone be able to fix it. Panic threatens to take over, stealing my breath. Can I even *do* this?

"Earth to Wren," Evianna says, oblivious to my distress. "You want some cider?"

I startle, and my heart thuds against my chest so hard, I can *hear* it. "Sorry. Cider would be great."

She snags two glasses from Cara, sinks down next to me, and nudges my shoulder with hers. "You've been spacey since I got here. Did you have another panic attack this morning?"

"No. Not today." The worst part of pregnancy? Not the nausea. Or the cankles. Or the stretch marks. It's the panic attacks. My daily anxiety medication is safe enough to take, but the pill that can calm my panic attacks is too risky. Deep breathing only takes me so far. Or...not very far at all.

I rub my side. There's usually a tiny hand over there somewhere. Can Harlow tell the difference between my touch and Ry's? Does she know he talks to her every night before bed? That he sleeps with his hand on my belly?

"Then what is it?" Evianna angles her body between me and the rest of the room and lowers her voice. "Are you feeling up to this today? Say the word and I'll get everyone out of here in less than ten minutes."

"Spitsnacks." I run my fingers through my hair. "No one needs to leave. I feel fine—physically. Or...as fine as I'm *supposed* to feel at thirty-nine weeks. But in just a few more days, there's going to be a little person depending on us—on me—for everything. She won't be able to talk. Or stand. Or tell me what's wrong. What if I'm...*bad* at this?"

"Oh, honey. You'll be a great mom," Evianna says as she wraps her arms around me. I fight the tears that have been threatening for days, blinking them back as quickly as I can.

Inara takes a seat across from us. "She's right. You've got this, Wren. Women have been having babies for centuries. But you have the power of the internet—and all of us. Though, I've never changed a diaper in my life. Or...shit... even held a baby before."

"Graham has a little experience with kids," Cara adds. "And Hope and I are only two floors down."

Tears burn my eyes. The crying is almost as bad as the constant need to pee. My hormones are on a see-saw. One that's spinning around in a circle as it goes up and down.

"We've got you, sugar. Whatever you need," Raelynn says, then shrugs—like she's regretting the offer. Or isn't sure she should have interrupted in the first place.

I swipe at my cheeks. "Then you're on backup beer duty. Can I trust you to pick a *good* beer?"

"Depends. You want Shiner Bock, Shiner Bock, or Shiner Bock?" She tosses me a wink before she studies the bottle of Pilsner and maybe...relaxes a fraction. We're growing on her.

CHAPTER TWO

Ryker

"GET A MOVE ON," West shouts as he checks his stopwatch. "Rip, you're going to be last if you don't pick up the pace."

"Fuck you," Ripper mutters. He passes the SEAL and raises his middle finger. This is his first official workout with the team, and West isn't taking it easy on him.

Graham cracks the seal on a bottle of water and drapes a towel over his shoulder. "Rip is gonna be in a world of hurt tomorrow," he says. "I remember my first session. I couldn't get out of bed the next day."

"He could just stop." As soon as I say the words, I know they're useless. Ripper won't stop until he passes out or West tells him he's done. He's spent two years trying to reclaim even a fraction of the man he used to be. The one who was captured with me and Dax. Back then, he could run a mile in under seven minutes. And hike for hours carrying a sixty-pound ruck. He's come so far, but though he tries to hide it, he gets dizzy spells. Too many traumatic brain injuries. Along with all the other shit he went through.

I cut my hand across my throat, giving West the signal to call it. We've been at this for three hours. The baby shower should be over soon, and we still have a hell of a lot of shit to hash out.

"That's good enough for today." The SEAL strides for the kitchen and a fresh cup of coffee. "Get yourself a good cool down, folks. Company meeting in thirty."

I head for the table where Dax sits with his tablet, using his VoiceAssist software to catch up on his email. "Want to go a couple of rounds in the ring?" I ask. "We've got a little time."

He taps the earbud and tilts his head so he's looking right at me—despite not being able to see much more than hazy shadows. "So I can kick your ass again? You sure you're up for that?"

"Put up or shut up, brother."

His rough chuckle should probably serve as a warning. I've got more than six inches and a hundred pounds on him, but Dax hits up his boxing gym back in Boston five days a week. Half the time, Ford joins him, and from what I hear, the older man almost never comes out on top.

Ten minutes later, Dax ducks between the ropes, wearing a pair of basketball shorts and a black t-shirt. I wish I didn't care so much about the scars that cover almost every inch of me. Though, maybe if I couldn't see them, I'd be more willing to wear something other than long sleeves and pants all the time.

"You ready?" he asks as he flexes his fingers to test the wraps around his knuckles. "Because you can still chicken out. I won't hold it against you. Much."

He flashes a sly smile, and I see a hint of the man I knew all those years ago.

"Not on your life." I bounce on the balls of my feet, watching for any sort of tell. Years ago, he'd drop his left shoulder a split second before he threw a jab.

We circle each other, and Dax's gaze, though unfocused, darts from side to side. His right hand twitches, and I spin away. His cross comes within an inch of my jaw. "Not bad," he says. "For a guy who can see."

I deflect another hit—this one headed for my chin—and land a punch to his solar plexus. He coughs, and I freeze for a split second. Long enough for him to sweep his leg out and catch me behind the ankles.

My ass hits the deck. Rolling onto my knees, I spring up and lunge for him. But my fingers find only the hem of his t-shirt. "You've got some speed. I'll give you that. But I'm stronger."

"Strength isn't everything," he grunts after I send him spinning into the ropes. He uses the momentum, tucks and rolls, and scissors his legs around my knees. "Creativity helps."

I land on my back, and the air leaves my lungs in a *whoosh*. "Fuck."

"That's two for two." He leans down and offers me his hand. "Though seems like the SEAL taught you a few things since the last time we sparred."

"I've still never beaten him," I grumble as I let him help me to my feet, wincing when my knees protest. Arthritis is a son of a bitch, and after spending fifteen months bound in various stress positions, beaten on the regular, with no medical care, I'll never be whole. None of us will be.

"Are the two of you done?" West shouts from one of the couches in the sitting area. "Inara and Raelynn will be here in ten minutes. Time to do this thing."

"SHE'S FINE, RY." Inara angles her phone so I can see the picture of Wren holding a green onesie so tiny, I can't believe it'll actually fit our daughter—even as a newborn. "Cara had to go to the restaurant for a few hours, but Evianna's staying with her."

I nod, then stand and shove my hands into my pockets. "This isn't a conversation I ever thought I'd have."

Dax doesn't meet my gaze, but one by one, every other member of Hidden Agenda does. They all know what's coming. We've danced around the subject for weeks. Months, even. Hell, I didn't go to Boston with the rest of the team when Zephyr was taken. And I stayed in the van in Salt Lake City while Wyatt went after Hope.

"Hidden Agenda gave me a purpose when I didn't know how to go on. When nothing made sense. When I didn't have anyone who cared about me." Dax's flinch is like a knife to my heart. I heave a sigh, my gaze on his even if he can't see it. "When I didn't *think* I had anyone who cared about me. But every time we go out on a job, there's a chance we won't come home. It never mattered much to me before I met Wren. And after...she understood. But it's not just her anymore."

I look to West. "Sampson's planned every op we've had since he joined. He's more than capable of running this team."

"What does that mean for...funding?" Inara asks. "Because West might be a fucking genius, but *my* investments do a hell of a lot better than his."

The SEAL shoots her a look. "I let Rip handle all my shit now."

"For fuck's sake," I mutter. "I'm not *dying*. Or going off the grid. Neither is Dax. Our financials are solid and they'll stay that way. I'm sticking close to home. It might be temporary, it might be permanent. And Wren...she can't be our go-to tech resource anymore." Turning to Ripper, I wait for him to lift his gaze to mine. "You're on point, brother. If you're up for it."

Fear churns in his irises for a second, and he balls his

hands into fists. "Yeah. I can do it. But...is Zephyr going to help us out if we need it? The last few ops...Wren and I both had our hands full."

"When she can. She's been on a case for Austin for the past thirty-six hours," I say. "We're going to need to recruit for tech and ops." I look to Dax. "Unless someone from Second Sight wants to relocate?"

"I can ask. Ella might want a fresh start. But everyone else has family in Boston or close by," he says. "You're handling two or three jobs a month, Ry. On average. If you keep up this pace, you're going to wear everyone out. We need at least another five, six people. If not more. Otherwise, we can't—" his voice breaks, and he clears his throat, "—save everyone."

"The hell we can't."

He's right. I know he's right. But after spending fifteen months convinced we'd never taste freedom again, the idea of leaving *anyone* behind sickens me. Until the answer smacks me in the face.

"We need to expand."

"Are you losing your hearing?" Dax asks. "I just said that."

"My hearing's fine. We'll find one or two more folks to join us here in Seattle. But what we truly *need*?" I pause, sweeping my gaze over the men and women who've become my family. "Hidden Agenda locations around the world. South America. Europe. The Middle East. People we can trust in multiple countries. So when we take a job, we're not flying from Seattle to South Africa. Or hell, even France."

West nods. "That's...doable. Finding people we can trust will take some time, but if we could work it so no one's ever flying more than six hours? That'd be easier on everyone."

Why didn't I think about this sooner? We've been running ourselves ragged the past couple of years, and while we've saved a lot of people, we've had too many close calls. "Any objections to this plan?" I ask.

One by one, my team—my family—shakes their heads. "Then that's it. Sampson's in charge of things here. He's been running ops for three years anyway. I'll still be around. I'll come to workouts. If Wren doesn't need me at home. I can't do...nothing. And while Wren's not here, I guarantee she'll tell you the exact same thing. So once we've found our footing with the baby, we'll handle recruiting—along with Dax and Pritchard. Any questions?"

Raelynn stands, and I arch a brow. She's still not putting all her weight on her injured leg. Fuckers who were after Nash a month ago almost killed her before West, Inara, and I got to her house and put an end to them. "You got something to say, probie?"

She shoots Wyatt a pointed look. "I keep tellin' you. I ain't the probie anymore. *He* is."

"He's backup. Unless he's changed his mind," West says.

Wyatt shakes his head. "Not yet. Hope still needs me. Even if she didn't, I'll never be a hundred percent again. You don't want me on mission unless there's no other option."

"Fine." Raelynn huffs out a breath. "I'll be the goddamn probie from now until the end of time. Happy now?"

"Wyatt is. Say your piece, *probie*."

She looks vaguely uncomfortable. "Ry, you—and West—gave me a chance when I didn't know which way was up. I'd follow all y'all to the ends of the earth if you asked. No one here's gonna give you shit for stickin' close to home. You found all of us. Brought us together and made us...a family. We've got your back."

CHAPTER THREE

Ripper

CHARLIE NUDGES MY HAND, then trots over to sit in front of the door. I'm wiped after actually trying to participate in one of Hidden Agenda's workout sessions, but the German Shepherd spent all afternoon lazing about in his dog bed at the warehouse. He's got energy to burn.

"I know, I know. Too much working and too little walking."

When he first came home with me from Safe Haven Animal Shelter, we'd spend hours outside. Walking down to Green Lake, sitting for a while, walking some more. Five, seven miles in a day wasn't unusual. Walls—even here in the sanctuary I've found with Cara—were my enemy. The only way I could spend *any* time inside was to spend as much time as possible *outside*.

And Charlie loved it. But the past few months...they've been hard. Hope's kidnapping, Raelynn and Nash squaring off with the Chicago mob, a couple of tricky K&R cases I handled because Wren just can't work eighteen-hour days as pregnant as she is...

I push to my feet, sway, and brace myself against the arm of the couch. Six fucking years as Faruk's punching bag, and the lingering effects of too many traumatic brain injuries still leave me unsteady if I get up too quickly or push myself too hard. Ry keeps telling me to see a neurologist, but what the fuck are they going to do? Run a shit-ton of tests and tell me to live with it? No, thank you.

Charlie whines and presses himself to my legs. "I'm okay, buddy. Just need a second." He stares up at me, his head cocked. With one of his ears half mangled, he looks perpetually curious, like he's always trying to figure out what I might need next, or what I want him to do.

But he doesn't need to figure it out. He just knows. Has since the first time I met him. "Come on. Let's get your leash."

He practically prances back to the door. I pat my pockets, making sure I have my cell phone. Cara had to run to the restaurant to prep for tomorrow's breakfast rush, and I haven't seen her since I left for the warehouse more than six hours ago. I wish I could feel her arms around me right now.

You could walk up to the restaurant and see her.

She'd understand. But after two years, I should be...better. One hard workout shouldn't leave me feeling so...off balance. But it does. Or maybe it's the conversation Ry had with all of us before we called it a day. The one about what's going to happen now that Ry and Wren can't drop everything on a moment's notice to work a job.

We'd put off that "talk" for too long already. I knew it was coming—even knew *what* was coming—but I still wasn't ready. My hands shake at the thought of going on mission without Ry.

At my side, Charlie whines and nudges my hip. How long have I been standing here, lost in my own thoughts? Too long. I clip the leash to his collar and run my fingers through the fur on the back of his neck. "I've got two miles in me, buddy. Let's burn off some of that energy."

The hall is completely silent. There are only three units on this floor. Graham and Q are on our left, Wyatt and Hope on our right. Ry bought this building not long after he pulled me out of that fucking well in Afghanistan and retrofitted it with the best security money can buy. We're safe here. While the first four levels are home to a few local businesses and live-work units, Wren vets every single tenant. And *no one* gets past the fifth floor without a keycard, palm print, voice code, and retinal scan.

The elevator doors snick shut, trapping me and Charlie inside. For over a year, I took the stairs every damn time. But *normal* people don't walk down—and up—six flights every time their dog needs to take a piss.

My palms are damp by the time I escape into the building lobby. But Charlie's so excited to see the street, I can almost forget how my heart pounded against my ribs the whole ride down.

The air holds the promise of summer, though it's only the end of April. Charlie sniffs every tree, and I keep watch for threats—despite this being a safe neighborhood. The condo isn't in my name. The one I was born with *or* the fake one I adopted when Ry and Dax rescued me. Rick Mercury has a P.O. Box downtown, but that's it. Otherwise, he's just as much of a ghost as Jackson Richards.

Charlie does his business, looks up at me, and then tugs gently on his leash. "Ready to put a mile or two on those paws?"

He yips, and I give him a nod. "Lead the way, buddy."

An hour later, my legs are ready to give out, but he's loving life so much, I hate to disappoint him. But if I don't get off my feet soon, I'll be in a world of hurt. "Time to turn around." He whines, clearly disappointed in me. That's the only explanation for his good ear flattening against his head and the sorrowful look in his eyes.

I drop down to one knee and ruffle his fur. "You're right. I spend too much time at the warehouse and not enough time walking. We'll find a better balance soon. Okay?"

He agrees with me. At least that's what I hope his happy bark means. We're two miles from the condo, and it takes me several minutes to convince him we're going home. Eventually, I bribe him with the promise of treats. Cara always tells him he's "the best dog ever" before she gives him one, and as soon as I say those words, he's practically trotting toward home.

When I code myself back into the condo, I find Cara curled up on the couch, her eyes closed. Charlie bounds over to her and noses her hand.

"Hey, buddy," she says as she stretches her arms over her head. "Guess I need to get up now, huh?"

"Stay there, sunshine." I shuffle over to the treat jar and toss him a biscuit. "Good boy. We'll get more exercise tomorrow."

"How far did you go?" Cara asks. She sits up, stifling a yawn. "It's almost dark."

"Four miles. Give or take." My left knee cracks as I sink down next to her. "West is a fucking sadist."

Cara's laugh eases all my aches and pains. "You said you were going to take it easy."

"I had to know..."

"Know what?" She snuggles closer to me, draping her legs over my thighs.

"If I could still do it." I twine my fingers with hers. "Ry had the talk with everyone today. He's handing Hidden Agenda over to West. At least operationally."

"That wasn't a surprise, though," she says, stroking her thumb over mine. "He won't want to leave Wren and the baby."

"No. And he shouldn't. It's not just that, though. He's looking to expand. Have teams all around the world. But that takes time. A lot of it. Until he can recruit—and vet—all new people…"

My chest tightens, and the walls start to close in on me. It's dark outside the floor-to-ceiling windows. So very dark.

Cara slides her hand up to the back of my neck. "Jackson, you're safe. At home. With me."

Fuck. She calms me like no one else can. Makes me feel safe when nothing else in my life makes sense. I rest my forehead against hers and let myself feel. Getting *through* is the only way to escape the memories threatening to pull me under.

"What if they need me to go on mission again?" I whisper. "I was lucky when we had to rescue Hope. But that was mostly Ry's doing. Next time, I might not be able to stay in the van."

Cara pulls back enough to hold my gaze. "Then you'll get out of the van. And you'll protect your brothers and sisters—and whoever you're there to rescue—because that's who you are."

CHAPTER FOUR

Wren

"No. The last time you came with me, the poor ladies at the salon were so scared, Daria dropped her grandmother's teapot and it shattered into a million pieces."

Ry's shoulders jerk halfway up to his ears for a brief moment before he mutters, "I tried to buy her a new one."

I roll my eyes. "You know that's not the same thing." I push up the sleeve of the *tent-of-the-day*—aka the only maternity clothes I can wear at almost forty weeks—and run my fingers over the fluorite beads around my wrist. "Would you buy me an exact replica of my bracelet if it broke?"

He sighs, conceding my point. "No. But I don't like the idea of you going alone."

"I won't be alone. Evianna and Cara will be with me the whole time. It's only three blocks away. I'm pregnant. Not a ticking time bomb."

His jaw hardens, and a vein at his temple throbs. "That's exactly what you are." He drops to his knees in front of me, framing my belly with his hands. "Your due date is in two days. You could go into labor any time."

"Even if I do, you'll be able to reach me, soldier." I cup his cheek. "You can always reach me."

———

EVIANNA WIGGLES her bright red toes as she stretches in the massage chair. "God, I needed this. I hired a new CTO for Beacon Hill Technologies last month. Once she's fully up to speed, she'll be able to take a lot of work off my plate. But until then...I'm doing my job *and* part of hers."

"I wish we'd had time to book massages," Cara says and closes her eyes. "I made two hundred Pop Tarts after the breakfast rush this morning, and my shoulders are killing me."

I take a sip of herbal tea and admire my glittering purple nails. "I've only had a massage once in my life. It...didn't go well."

"How does a massage not 'go well'?" Evianna asks.

My cheeks flush. "I had a panic attack on the table."

"Why? Did something trigger you?" She presses a button on the chair remote to turn the vibrations down and drains the last of her sparkling wine.

Though the three of us are close—almost as close as sisters now—I don't talk about my panic disorder very often. I shrug. "Nothing I know of. There isn't always a reason though. Mani-pedis are about all the pampering I can handle."

On the other side of me, Cara stifles another squeal. Apparently, she's ticklish, and the poor young woman painting her toes barely managed to escape a kick to the chin when she tried to scrub Cara's instep.

Cara runs a hand through her dark locks. "I love you,

Wren, but this is my first and last pedicure."

"I know I'm one to talk," Evianna says, "but the two of you really need to learn how to relax."

I almost choke on my tea. "Says the woman who worked all morning and has been answering texts every twenty minutes."

"Only two of those were from work. The other two...well, the Five Points remodeled last month. The furniture isn't the same, and the whole place is a mess. Dax is having a hard time. Apparently housekeeping left the chair pulled out and moved everything on the bathroom counter." She shows us her phone—and the photo of their toiletries shoved into a corner behind the sink.

Despite working with Dax for years, I never stopped to think how hard it must be for him to travel. Yes, he's blind. But he navigates the world better than half the sighted people I know. Better than me most days.

Her phone buzzes again, and after a few seconds, her cheeks are almost as red as her nails.

"Evianna?" Cara asks. "Oh, my God. Is Dax...sexting you?"

"I can't think about Dax sexting. He's my boss!" I avert my eyes, pinning my gaze to one of the ceiling tiles as Evianna types out a quick response.

"Well, I *could* tell you what happened after the baby shower last night," she says.

"Nope. Unless it involved being able to see your feet, tie your shoes, or go more than twenty minutes without peeing. Those are the only fantasies I'm interested in right now."

Daria finishes the last coat of polish on my toes and pats my calf. "You're done, love. But wait at least ten minutes before you get up. And..." She peers up at me, narrowing her eyes like she knows something I don't. "Stay close to home on Friday. It's a new moon. I think your daughter will come then."

I gape at her. "I never said I was having a girl. Did I?"

She chuckles. "I've had five children and sixteen nieces and nephews. I can tell." Waving her hand, she motions for the teapot. "I can also tell you're dehydrated. Have more tea."

"Well, that was weird," Cara says when the three of us are alone again. "And maybe a little creepy."

"It happens everywhere. Apparently, it's a thing." The light, floral taste of the tea is comforting. Will I really have this kid in just three days?

"A thing?" Evianna swings her legs over the side of the massage chair. "What's a thing?"

"Random people thinking because you're pregnant, they can touch your belly or give you unsolicited parenting advice. Some woman in the grocery store a couple of weeks ago told me all about breastfeeding and how the only good nipple cream was made out of—well, trust me. You don't want to know."

Cara frowns. "Who the hell does that?"

"According to the internet, everyone." I drain the last of the tea and shrug. "I have a lot of downtime while I'm running code. And I don't know anyone with kids. So I signed up for a couple of pregnancy message boards."

I shouldn't feel guilty about my admission, but Evianna and Cara are my two closest friends. And I've kept this from them for...well...almost nine months.

"Ry doesn't know," I say. "About the woman at the grocery store. Don't tell him, okay? He doesn't want me going anywhere alone. Heck, he tried to come with us today. He wanted to sit in the lobby for two hours and glare at everyone who came through the doors."

"Daddy McCabe is going to be a force to be reckoned with," Evianna says with a smile.

My eyes fill with tears, and the room starts to shimmer.

"Hey," Cara says, reaching over to rest her hand on mine.

"What's wrong?"

"I'm not going to lose...me...when I have the baby? Am I?"

Suddenly, I'm sobbing. Evianna and Cara's arms come around me, and all I can think is that they're going to ruin their pedicures because clearly they're not listening to Daria and keeping their toes under the little fans.

"You're not going to lose yourself," Evianna says softly. "You ran comms while hunched over the toilet with morning sickness. You wrote code waiting for the ultrasound technician. You're so hardwired to be *you*, nothing will ever change that."

"Fudgesicles. I'm going to be a terrible mom." Even as I say the words, I hear how ridiculous they sound, but I can't stop myself. "What if I can't find the right balance? I've stayed up for thirty-six hours working before. I can't do that with a baby. But if I don't work, people could die. Ripper and Zephyr are amazing, but I can do things they can't. And there isn't time to teach them before Friday!"

"Wren, look at me." Evianna's sharp tone is enough for me to sniffle and swipe at my cheeks. "Rip and Z *are* great. But you're not going to the moon. You're having a baby. Pretty sure you can still talk on the phone while breastfeeding. Or changing a diaper. You'll still be a part of the team. Just one who carries a binky and knows all the words to Twinkle, Twinkle, Little Star."

"Doesn't everyone know that song?" I manage. "It's like...a classic."

We share a laugh, and a fraction of the weight I've been carrying for months lifts from my shoulders. If only my ankles felt the same relief. I miss being able to walk comfortably. Sit comfortably. Do *anything* comfortably.

"You're going to be fine, hon," Evianna says. "I promise."

Our flip-flops slap against the sidewalk. That's the problem with pedicures. You can't wear real shoes for hours—if you want the polish to last. And since I probably won't have the time—or energy—to make another salon appointment for months...I'm playing it safe.

"I need arch support," Evianna says on a sigh. "When you wear heels every day..."

"Oh, God. You're the boss. Wear what's comfortable. Heels are pure torture." I shudder at the very idea of spending my days in anything but Keds, Sketchers, or slippers. With my anxiety, Ryker and I don't go out much. We're takeout and Netflix people. Not dinner and dancing people. And I wouldn't change a thing.

Except, the baby is about to change everything. Bedtime stories, diaper changes, feedings... My chest tightens as the first stirrings of overwhelm wash over me. If I'm not careful, I'll end up having a panic attack, and I don't want to ruin such a lovely afternoon.

The traffic signal changes as we reach the curb, and I brace a hand on the small of my back. Walking isn't exactly comfortable, but standing is a hundred times worse.

A bell jingles from the florist shop to my left, and I glance at the windows full of colorful bouquets. In the reflection, a man across the street stares at us. I only notice because he isn't moving. At all. And despite the warmth of the late April day, he's dressed all in black, including a knit cap pulled all the way down to his dark sunglasses.

I'm no longer overwhelmed. I'm worried. Shivering, even with the sun shining down on us, I loop my fingers around the crook of Cara's elbow. "Can you do me a favor?"

"Anything. Well, except sign up for another pedicure." She laughs and squeezes my hand. "I love you, Wren, but my self-preservation instinct is really strong."

I pass her my phone and turn us so our back is to the guy

across the street. "Take a picture of the three of us."

She frowns at me. "Wren, I can't put any pictures on social media. It's too dangerous. And you don't even like getting your picture taken."

"It's not a 'real' selfie. There's a guy across the street watching us. I think I saw him outside the salon too. I need a photo of him."

Evianna sucks in a sharp breath and starts to turn, but I hiss at her, "Don't! If he runs, we won't have any idea what he looks like. Please. Play along."

Though they both urge me to call Ry immediately, I hold the phone up to get a good angle of the three of us. Or...I make it look that way. Because my arms are too short to get a decent shot.

After a few attempts, Cara eases the device from my hand and turns it on its side. "Smile, ladies," she calls out—a little louder than necessary. After a couple of clicks, she taps the screen again and slowly lowers the phone. "I tried to catch a video too. But the resolution might not be the best."

The light changes, the happy chirping of the walk signal at odds with the strain we're all feeling.

"We can't go back to the condo," Evianna says as we cross the street. "Call Ry. Get him to meet us somewhere."

"What about that bar on Seneca?" Cara asks. "They have a bouncer all day long. It's only a few blocks away."

"That'll be good." I dig in my purse and find my Bluetooth earbud. "Is he still back there?"

Evianna lets out a laugh and executes a truly brilliant—and graceful—three-hundred-and-sixty-degree spin. To anyone else, she looks like she's having a great time with her friends. But I can see the fear in her eyes.

"Yes. I think he's texting. But he's definitely keeping pace with us."

"Spitsnacks. Ry's going to bust a gasket."

CHAPTER FIVE

Ryker

When I walk into the bar, it only takes me seconds to find Wren, Evianna, and Cara. They're at a table against the wall with a full view of the door. Smart.

A plate of fries sits untouched in front of them. To anyone else, they look like they're having fun. But at my side, Ripper swears under his breath. He sees it. Cara's hands clenched under the table. Wren's glassy eyes. Evianna twisting her wedding ring around her finger.

"Sir, we don't allow dogs." A guy with bright blue hair tucks a pair of menus under his arm. "You can tie him up outside."

"He stays. You got a problem with that?" I ask, hands on my hips.

"N-no. Sit...anywhere," he stammers and backs away.

Rip shakes his head. "Way to make the kid piss himself, Ry."

"You're welcome." By the time I reach the table, Wren's on

her feet, and I wrap my arms around her. "You okay, little bird?" She nods against my chest.

Ripper pulls Cara close, and Charlie presses to her thighs. After a beat, he sidles up to Evianna and noses her hand. The dog is more perceptive than half the guys I went through Basic with.

"We didn't see anyone suspicious on the way here," I say. "But Graham's outside, keeping watch. We're taking a nice leisurely walk down to the waterfront, where West will pick us up. We're not going back to the condo until we're *sure* we're not being followed."

"You told Dax what happened?" Evianna asks.

"I sent a car to your hotel to pick him up. He's already at the condo, waiting for us."

She sags against the table and swipes at her eyes.

Wren's trembling, and I tip her chin up so I can brush a kiss to her lips. "Rip and Zephyr can go to work on traffic camera footage once we get back. If there's anything to find..."

"I know. They'll find it. *We'll* find it," she says and straightens her shoulders. "I should have let you come with us. You'd have seen him before I did. But this was the last time..." Tears swim in her eyes.

Fuck. I don't know how to reassure her. Or if I even can. "It's *not* the last time, sweetheart. For anything. We're having a baby. Not moving to the Arctic Circle. Once we figure out who the guy is and why he was following you, I'll put an end to him—to it."

Wren sniffles once, then offers me a weak smile. "No, you meant him. You forget I know you, Ry."

She's not wrong.

Outside, Graham takes Evianna's arm. The kid's a damn good actor, staring down at her like she's his entire world. I'd feel better if Wyatt were with us too, but he took Hope to her physical therapy session an hour ago.

Ripper, Cara, and Charlie take the lead. The German Shepherd is on high alert, feeding off Rip's anxiety. The shelter he volunteers at didn't know where the dog came from when he showed up a couple of years ago with a mangled ear and no chip, but I'd bet a hell of a lot of money he was trained as a police or military dog.

Evianna laughs at something Graham says, though her shoulders are approximately half a centimeter from her ears. I can't focus on Wren. Not completely. Not and scan for threats. But I feel her worry.

She doesn't spook easily. Never has. So whoever the asshole is? He's dead.

"You're thinking so hard, I'm surprised there isn't a thought bubble floating over your head." She digs her fingers into my side. "Spit it out."

"Not yet." This conversation can't happen out on the street. Or without Dax. "When we're home. With the door locked."

"You're not making me feel any better," she mutters. "And the door is *always* locked."

Well, fuck. I've always been shit at reassuring her. Reassuring *anyone*. And we're about to have a baby.

Our daughter will need me to tell her she's safe. Protected. Loved.

What if I can't do it? What if I try and she doesn't believe me?

Wren glances up at me, and damn. She can see it. Everything. My worry. The panic that hasn't disappeared since the day she told me she was pregnant.

"Breathe, Ry. If I can, you can."

For her, I can try. But we're still two blocks from the waterfront. I haven't seen anyone following us, and my phone peeks out of my back pocket, recording everything behind us. Rip has a camera clipped to his belt buckle to capture the street ahead of us. We didn't have time to fit Graham with a device, but he's perceptive well beyond his years. He might not have my memory—yet—but he's getting there.

My phone buzzes, and I check the screen.

West: I'm in the Pike Place garage. Slot B-23. All clear down here.

"Sampson's ready for us," I say. "Let's go home."

TWENTY MINUTES LATER, we're in the elevator up to the eighth floor of the building I bought when Ripper decided to move to Seattle. The security is beyond top of the line. The garage needs a keycard, fingerprint scan, and an eighteen-digit access code. The elevator uses a second access code, a voice print, and—to reach the sixth, seventh, and eighth floors—a retinal scan.

The six of us—plus Charlie—ride all the way to the top. As soon as the elevator doors open, Wren rushes ahead of me to our condo. "I really have to pee," she says, a bright red flush to her cheeks. "I didn't want to risk going at the bar."

I don't say a word as she beelines for the bathroom.

Dax, who's been in my living room for the past half an hour, stands. "Evianna?" Behind his tinted glasses, his eyes search her out, though I doubt he can tell her and Cara apart. They're almost the same height.

Yet he crosses to her without hesitation, and Evianna wraps her arms around his waist.

"You okay, darlin'?"

"Fine. The guy...he was just watching. Creepy, but he didn't approach us."

"Watching all of you? Or Wren?" Dax asks. From the edge

to his voice, he's barely holding it together. So am I, if I'm honest. But I can't lose my shit. Not now.

"I don't know," Evianna says. "We stopped to 'window shop' a couple of times, and he seemed like he was focused on Wren, but we stuck close together, so it was hard to tell."

Wren trudges back into the room, Pixel winding around her ankles and yipping the whole way. As soon as she sinks into the recliner, the pup scrambles up next to her and settles across her lap. She twines her fingers through the dog's curls. "We got a photo of him. Kind of."

"What?" Dax, Rip, and I ask in tandem.

"I made Cara take some selfies of the three of us. She got a video too." Pulling out her phone, she unlocks it and offers it to me.

Rip reaches over and plucks the device from my hand. "Grainy. But workable."

"I sent it to my system when we were at the bar. Facial rec should already be working on it." She stifles a yawn. "But Rip could start running it against the traffic cameras. See if the guy has been anywhere near the condo in the past few weeks. I haven't seen him before today. At least not that I know of."

"He looks..." I peer over Rip's shoulder. "Afghan. Pakistani. Maybe Uzbek."

"Fuck." Dax stalks over to the window and presses his hands to the glass. Sunlight streams into the main room this time of day, and he can feel it. Maybe even see it—a little. "So why is he here? He better not have any fucking friends in town."

"Wouldn't that be worse?" Wren asks. "If he doesn't have any reason to be here? Because then...he's here for me. Or you."

"There's no fucking way he's here for us." I straighten my shoulders and run a hand over my bald head. "Because we don't exist."

"I do." Dax turns back to us. "Second Sight is in my name. You and Rip are ghosts, but I've been out in the open this whole time. What if this asshole is related to the guys in Turkey."

"He's not. Trust me. Trust West and his...methods." I cut my gaze to Rip. There's no way I'm going to tell Dax how that op went down in front of him. He's better now. But I worry every goddamn day that one bad memory will send him spiraling.

"For fuck's sake. Will you stop looking at me like that?" Ripper pushes off the wall and stalks over to me. "You want me to take on more work for Hidden Agenda? I'm going to have to hear this shit. I can handle it, Ry. And if I can't, that's on me to let you know."

"He's right," Dax says quietly. "You and Wren are going to have a kid any day now. Pritchard has so much work for Zephyr, he'll be hiring soon. We *need* Rip. Unless you've figured out a way to clone Wren..."

My little bird barely manages to stifle her yawn. "Flippin' flapjacks. That would be the best thing ever. I'd be able to sleep. Even with a newborn."

"You're exhausted." I kneel next to the recliner and cup her cheek. "I'm putting you to bed."

"You'll do no such thing," she says sharply, but leans into my touch like I'm the only thing keeping her upright. "I can make it to the bedroom on my own."

She must be completely wiped out to agree with me. "I know you *can*, sweetheart." Lowering my voice, I press a kiss to her temple. "Let me do this. Please."

With a nod, she lets me scoop the dog off her lap and help her up. "Evianna, lunch tomorrow? Here?"

"Name the time." Evianna links her fingers with Dax's. "We'll be here."

IN OUR BEDROOM, I pull back the blankets, then drop to one knee to help her off with her flipflops. "Purple. I like it."

"Had to do something that didn't scream, 'Mom,'" she says. "If I weren't worried about the chemicals, I'd dye my hair purple too."

God, I wish I knew what to say to her. To promise neither of us will lose ourselves to being parents. That we'll still be "Wren and Ry." Not just "Mom and Dad."

But it's been my second—or third—biggest fear. Behind something happening to her or the baby, or our daughter taking one look at me and screaming her head off for days because she thinks I'm a monster.

Even if I did have the right words, though, now isn't the time. She's already curled around her body pillow, her eyelids drooping.

"I want to give the seventh floor to Dax and Evianna."

"What?" She pushes up on an elbow, her eyes only slightly more open now. "Like...for them to move out here?"

"Not full time." I glance back at the door, wishing I'd thought to bring this up before now. "Their lives are in Boston. Evianna's mom, Beacon Hill Technologies... But they're out here every four to six weeks. And every time, Dax has to manage the hotel, a car service, restaurants..."

"The Five Points remodeled," she says. "Evianna told me today. Dax hates it. Nothing's in the same place, half the housekeeping staff left, things keep getting moved in their room... It'll be nice having them here. Close by. They can set things up however they want and it'll always be the same. And they won't need a car service on standby until midnight just so we can have dinner."

I lean down and kiss her. If we had more time, I'd peel off

her tunic and show her how much I need her. How much I need *us*.

"I love you, Wren. So fucking much. I hope you know that."

"I do." Her lips part, and her breathy sigh has my dick straining against my briefs. "Make sure we have at least a couple of hours alone tonight, okay?"

"I promise."

CHAPTER SIX

Dax

EVIANNA CURLS against me on the couch, her head resting on my shoulder. Rip and Cara went back to their place so he could start checking the traffic camera footage for any evidence of the guy who tailed the women. Graham went home too. And Sampson never came up with them. He had a Krav Maga class to teach at his dojo.

"You doin' okay?" I ask.

"Jet-lagged," she says on a sigh. "And I hate the Five Points' new beds."

"They're too soft." More than once over the past few nights, I'd thought about moving to the couch in our hotel suite, but then I wouldn't have her in my arms, and I'm not sure I could sleep a wink without her. "Maybe we should look into getting a place out here. Something small. If we found a studio—"

"I have a better idea," Ryker says from behind us. "Though I'm a little pissed you stole my thunder."

He takes a seat across from us, and with the sun shining

through the windows, I can make out his silhouette. Mostly. "What are you talking about?"

"The seventh floor is empty. I can have it converted in a month. At most. Maybe less. You can't tell me you *like* staying at the Five Points all the time."

"I hate it—*we* hate it," I say. "Housekeeping is banned from the room because they've been moving all the shit on the counters. Pretty sure someone stole a couple of my Imitrex last time we were here too."

"And the beds are awful," Evianna adds.

"Then I should call the contractor?" Ry's voice holds more hope than I've heard in months. He's been so worried about becoming a father, he hasn't let himself relax since Wren found out she was pregnant.

Evianna squeezes my hand, and I nod. "Do it. But I'm paying for it."

"Dax—"

"I mean it. You're about to have a baby. Put whatever you were planning on spending for the renovation into Harlow's college fund. In eighteen years, Harvard will be up to half a million dollars a year."

"Harvard?" He chuckles, the sound a hell of a lot less raspy than it used to be. Proof we're not the same men we were when he strong-armed his way back into my life after six years. "You're so sure she'll want to go to college in Boston?"

"That's where her cool aunt and uncle live. Part time, anyway. That and any kid with both your DNA and Wren's is going to be a goddamn genius."

"Then she can go to MIT," Evianna says. Her warm fingers flutter over mine. "Like I did. She'll practically be a legacy."

"Are you sure?" Ry leans forward—I think, as the angle of his voice changes. "Footing the bill for the renovations."

"Yes. I did pretty damn well for myself in the six years you had your head up your ass. And Second Sight has a couple of clients who keep us on retainer and rarely ask us to do anything but run background checks."

Despite how close we've become in the three years since Ry burst into my office and offered me an olive branch, we don't talk about Second Sight much. I think he feels guilty I had to turn to Ford as my partner. That it should have been him.

He might be right. But without Ford, without the shit Joey went through in Afghanistan, we never would have found Ripper. Cara would probably be dead. He might have regrets, but I know we're all right where we're supposed to be.

"Let me do...something," he says quietly.

"Oh, you'll do plenty. Like finding us someone you're willing to let into this fortress to clean. Unless you're going to mop the floor on the regular."

"Fuck no. I have a company I've vetted."

My brows shoot up. "Wait. You let someone besides your team into this condo?" I turn to Evianna. "Something's wrong with Ry, darlin'. This whole baby thing broke his brain."

"I don't let them in here alone," he says with a huff. "And they aren't allowed in the bedroom. The hardline and the safe are in there."

Evianna laughs. "He's fine. The same paranoid grump we've come to know and love."

My phone buzzes, and the clipped, British voice announces, "Text from...Ford. Text from...Ford."

"Voice Assist, read text message."

"Message reads: 'Got a situation with the Boston Medical Research Fund. Vasquez and Tank have been working a case for the past three days, and shit just went sideways. Can you be available for a call in ten minutes?'"

I pull off my glasses and pinch the bridge of my nose. I

knew I should have asked Ronan to work with the two junior associates on this one. But it *should* have been a simple job.

"You can use Wren's office," Ry says. "All the rooms are soundproofed. After that, we can go check out the seventh floor."

"Thanks." I turn and slide my fingers into Evianna's hair. "I don't know how long I'll be. Do you want to go back to the hotel?"

"God, no," she says. "I have my tablet. I can work from here. We're still having dinner together tonight?"

"Yeah, but I'll order in." Ry stands, his large frame casting a dark shadow over the couch. "Until we figure out who was following Wren today, I'm not taking any chances."

Ripper

Charlie stops to sniff a tree and lifts his leg.

"Again? That's the fifth time in an hour."

He stares up at me, his tongue hanging half out of his mouth, happier than he's been in a while. We've walked at least four miles every day this week. I'm exhausted.

I stayed up half the night sifting through traffic camera footage, and even with Wren's help, we don't have anything more than a handful of grainy photos of the guy who followed her from the salon the other day.

No hits from any of the databases we can access. Connor hooked us up with one of his FBI contacts, but all we got from Brent was a very unhelpful, "Looks like the dude doesn't want to be found."

After another five blocks, Charlie stops short, his good ear standing straight up, and his body rigid. A low sound rumbles in his throat. Not quite a growl, but not his normal, inquisitive yip either.

I scan the street. It's the middle of the day. Just after the lunch hour. A group of business men exit one of the nicer restaurants in the area and cross in front of me. A mother pushes a stroller past me. Shoppers, tourists, commuters...

Tightening my grip on Charlie's leash, I follow his gaze to the corner. "Recon," I say quietly. He knows that word. I worked with him for months after Cara was kidnapped. He starts sniffing the air, and I give him a little more lead.

We turn onto the next block. It's quieter here. The sun doesn't penetrate the tall buildings, and the temperature drops a good ten degrees. A door slams, and I jump. "Fuck. Get a grip. It's the middle of the day."

Except, we still don't know if someone is after Wren, Ry, or all of us. Charlie barks, then strains against my hold. He's caught the scent of *something* he doesn't like.

We cover the length of the block in under a minute, but Charlie skids to a halt before we turn the corner. I almost crash into—and over—him.

"How much longer do we need to wait?"

Pashto. That's Pashto. I dart around my dog and burst out onto the sun-drenched sidewalk, searching for the man speaking a language I haven't heard since I left Afghanistan. But though a long line of cars backs up for several blocks, there are surprisingly few people on the street. A guy in a three-piece suit talks on his phone. It's not him. His accent is distinctly Irish. Two women in neon running gear chat about their latest dates. And a teenager bounces a basketball as he heads for the park on the corner.

I *know* what I heard. Charlie and I backtrack the way we came, then go over the same four city blocks three more times, but he doesn't alert over anything or anyone. I don't see anyone who *looks* suspicious. Who looks like they've been watching me.

Jackson Richards is dead. Killed in the Hindu Kush eight years ago. Officially, he was a victim of Hell Mountain and the sadistic fuck who ran it until Ry and Dax each put a bullet in his brain.

Wren has programs running twenty-four-seven that scan the internet—and the dark web—for any mention of my name. Of all our names.

She's the best. Better than me, and I'm a fucking genius with a computer. If she says no one knows I'm alive, no one knows I'm alive. At least no one online.

Charlie nudges my hand, and I stare down at him. He's worried. I'm close to losing my shit, and he's doing his damnedest to stop me. Closing his teeth over the sleeve of my jacket, he gives it a gentle tug. When I don't move, he whines, then tugs harder.

"Okay, okay." I drop down to one knee with a grunt and wrap an arm around his sleek body. "You're right. We need to go get Cara. Right now. Then we'll go home. Home is safe. No one can hurt us there."

I hope to God I'm right.

"WHAT IS IT?" Ry asks when he opens the door to his top-floor unit and sees me and Charlie in the hall.

His gaze holds a sea of worry, and I'm suddenly second guessing myself. What if it was just a random guy on vacation? Or someone working with one of those language apps?

"How's Wren?" She's not in the main room, and I know for a fact Ry isn't about to let her far out of his sight. Her due date was today.

"She's lying down. She had a couple of dizzy spells this

morning." He runs a hand over his shaved head, his shoulders slumping. "She swears she's fine. But I'd feel a hell of a lot better if she'd let me take her to the hospital."

"What can I do?"

He studies me for a beat. "Tell me what has you spooked."

Fuck. He was always the best of us at reading micro-expressions. A product of all those memory tricks he taught himself before we were captured. "It's nothing."

"We don't lie to each other, Rip. When you first came home, I let you get away with the little ones. All those times you told me you were okay when you weren't? But this...it's in your eyes. This is bigger."

I should have known he'd see right through me.

"So, spill it. Before I call Dax and tell him to get the fuck over here. Because right about now, he's probably having a nice dinner with Evianna."

Pixel trots into the room and drops one of her toys in front of Charlie. He glances up at me, and when I nod, grabs the stuffed bone and tosses it in the air for the little white puffball to catch.

"I heard someone speaking Pashto when I was walking Charlie this afternoon."

Ry's entire body tenses. "You're sure?"

Am I? Three hours ago, I would have bet my life on it. But after insisting Cara leave the restaurant early, locking myself in our condo, and scouring the traffic cameras in the area for hours, I'm not so sure.

"I didn't see the guy," I admit. "But..."

"Rip, you might not trust yourself anymore but I do. What did he say?"

"How much longer do we need to wait?"

Ry wasn't prepared for me to repeat the words in Pashto, and pain flashes through his multi-hued gaze.

"Sorry. I didn't...fuck. I *meant* to speak English." My eyes burn, and the lump in my throat makes it hard to breathe. Almost three years, and my broken mind still goes back there when I least expect it. Some days, I wake up expecting to see the bare, brown walls of the tiny room with the thin cot and the door that locked from the outside.

The scents of cardamom, coriander, and turmeric turn my stomach, and probably always will.

Charlie noses the hand balled into a fist at my side. Ry's meaty palm clamps down on my shoulder. "Look at me," he growls. "That's an order."

"I'm still...here," I say quietly as I snap my gaze to his. "Mostly."

He nods, and a muscle in his jaw flexes. "Seattle doesn't have a large Afghan population. In nine years, I've never heard a single person speaking Pashto. Urdu, sure. Arabic. Hindi. But not Pashto. It's too much of a coincidence after the guy following Wren the other day. If there's even a *possibility* someone from our past found us—any of us—we don't take chances. No one goes out alone until we figure this out. Got it? If Charlie needs to take a piss, you bring me or Graham with you."

CHAPTER SEVEN

Wren

I STIFLE a yawn from my recliner, push my lap desk away, and reach for the green smoothie on the side table. With a frown, I sniff it and set the glass back down. "Promise me, Ry. After this baby comes out, no more green smoothies. Ever."

He chuckles from the counter, where he's studying a thirty-second video I pulled off a security camera late last night. "I make no such guarantees, little bird. They're good for you."

I roll my eyes. "They're disgusting."

"I'll add more fruit. Less kale." Pressing a kiss to the top of my head, he peers down at the laptop screen. "Nothing?"

"My web crawlers haven't uncovered any chatter," I say. "If anyone were looking for you, I'd know. The last hit was more than eighteen months ago, and you put an end to those guys."

A vein in Ry's temple throbs. He took West, Inara, and Graham to Istanbul after someone spent a week searching for Ryker McCabe on the dark web. They fell into every trap I set for them. All the false leads. The tax records proving Ry was in Dallas, Texas. Then paperwork showing his move to Canada. Barcelona. New Delhi. And finally, Istanbul.

The three men they captured were related to the guards Ry killed when he escaped Hell Mountain. They lived for eight hours. Long enough for West to be sure they were acting alone. Their bodies were never found. Knowing my husband, they never will be.

He sinks down onto the couch, close enough I can reach for his hand and lay it on my belly. The baby's hiccupping, and it's the oddest sensation.

"If my darkness touches you or Harlow," he says, his voice barely more than a whisper, "I won't...I can't..."

I cover his fingers with mine. "Ry, our daughter isn't going to care that you have demons. She's only going to care that you love her."

His arms wind around me—so gently now that I'm about to pop—and in his embrace, I can breathe, despite the near-constant worry someone's after him.

"I can't lose you, Wren. I can't do this without you."

"This?" His eyes hold so much pain. More even than they did when we first met. "You're scaring me."

He stares out the floor-to-ceiling windows. The sun and gentle breeze turn Elliot Bay into a sea of glittering diamonds in the distance. "After Hell, I didn't know how I was going to survive in the world. There were days I didn't want to."

My heart aches for him. I try to wriggle closer, but my belly gets in the way.

"And then I met you. I don't think I'd laughed in six years. Or smiled. Or done a single fucking thing that wasn't absolutely necessary. I worked out. I ate. I slept—or tried to—and I saved people. I didn't talk to anyone outside of missions or training."

"Horsepucky."

He flinches and stares down at me. "Are you calling me a liar, sweetheart?"

"No. But you forget. I know you, Ryker McCabe. You read four books a week. At least. And that didn't start when you met me."

"Those are necessary."

Arching a brow, I snatch his phone from the coffee table, unlock it, and find his eReader app. "So, *Surprised and Sacked* is a necessary read?"

He huffs out a breath, and his cheeks take on a slight tinge. My big, hulking mountain of a husband who doesn't let a single thing knock him off his game is actually blushing.

"You read it last week. I...should know what you like."

I nestle against his side, enjoying the feel of his arm draped over my shoulders. "I love that about you." We sit in silence for several minutes, until I remember what started this whole conversation. "Ry, you can't be with me twenty-four hours a day. Even with West running Hidden Agenda. And what about when it's time for Harlow to go to preschool? Or college?"

The terror written all over his face makes my heart ache. This man who once thought he was too broken to care loves so deeply, with so much of his soul, he doesn't know how to put it into words.

"Remember what I told you when we first met?"

"You're going to have to be a little more specific there, little bird. I remember everything."

My lips curve into a smile. "Of course, you do." I sit up a little straighter and meet his gaze. "You said you didn't know how to care. And I said...?"

"You'll learn."

"Well, you'll learn how to do this too. How to trust that I'm okay. That our daughter's okay. Even when you can't see her. Or me."

"Not when there's a potential threat out there." It secretly thrills me that he's so protective he's practically growling. Even if it probably is overkill.

"We have a whole server farm running twenty-four-seven at the warehouse. None of the cameras we have around the building have picked up *anything*. Cara and Evianna are flippin' gorgeous. The guy who followed us was probably a creeper. And what Ripper heard…I don't know. I can't explain it."

The baby lands a hard kick to something vital, and I suck in a sharp breath. Ry tenses. "What hurts?"

"Nothing." I shake my head with a little chuckle. "Well, nothing more than everything. Your daughter is tired of these cramped accommodations. She'd like a two-bedroom apartment with a view and all the toys she can play with. And at least three more dogs."

As if she heard me talking about her, Pixel runs into the room. She drops down to her haunches in front of Ry, and her tail thumps against the rug so quickly, it's practically a blur.

"No, fur ball. You are not going out right now," he says. "You'll wait for Rip to come up in an hour."

"Take her. I'm fine. She hates sharing her walks with Charlie. He gets the best trees."

Ry stares at me for a long moment. "If you're sure…"

"You'll be gone fifteen minutes. Even if my water breaks, the baby won't come *that* quickly." I settle back on the couch and eye the smoothie glass.

"Okay, pipsqueak," he says. "Get your leash." Pixel runs to the door, noses her leash out of the toy basket, and drags it over to him. "But we are *not* dawdling. Understand?"

RYKER SLIPS BACK into the condo with Pixel trotting ahead of him like she just won the lottery. And she has, because he gave her a fancy new chew toy. He started buying them when I moved in with him, hides them, and brings them out at the oddest times.

"Who's a good girl?" I ask when she brings me the toy and drops it at my feet. "You're going to have to pick that up all on your own, sweet pea. Mama can't bend over right now. Maybe in another week or so, that'll change."

"Maybe?" Ry asks. "You don't think you'll still be pregnant in a week, do you?"

"No, but my stomach doesn't magically deflate when I give birth." I offer him a weak smile. "It might be months before I fit into my pre-pregnancy clothes."

The concern in his eyes touches me. "It's fine. But even after everything's...back the way it's supposed to be, I'm going to look different. My boobs won't ever be the same."

"Your breasts are perfect. Absolutely perfect." He cups one of them, dragging his thumb over my nipple.

"Fudgesicles," I moan with a shudder. "I've never been *this* sensitive. If I didn't have a doctor's appointment this afternoon, I'd say we get naked. Right now."

"We don't have to be at the medical center for two hours." He scoops me into his arms and carries me into the bedroom. "We have time."

"Ryker McCabe. Put me down right now!" I slap at his back, but it does me no good. Not that I want it to. The idea of one last roll in the sheets before the baby comes is more appealing than I can put into words. Who knows how long it's going to take before my body is ready to have sex again. Or my emotions.

Exhaustion. Worry. The idea of sex with a baby in the next room... At least we have a third bedroom now—one on the *other* side of the condo.

Ry lays me on the bed and shifts my long, blue maxi dress up my thighs.

I shiver, my nipples tight under my bra. Arousal floods my core. His black pants strain over his dick, and I unbuckle his belt. "Strip, soldier. I want you naked."

His black t-shirt falls to the floor. I'll never get tired of looking at him. At the ridges of muscles. The evidence of his strength over fifteen months of torture. His scars are a part of him. Some deep, some shallow—but no less painful. He remembers all of them. Every cut. Every burn. Every bone broken and set. But all that pain led him to me. Led *us* to this moment when we're about to start a family neither of us thought we'd ever have.

His pants are next. Black briefs can't hide the outline of his need. His thighs are as big as two of mine, and the veins... I could stare at him all day.

"Like what you see, sweetheart?" he rumbles.

"Oh, very much. But you're not naked yet. I'm not thrilled about that bit."

"Neither are you."

"True, but I'm on my back with a twenty-pound beach ball on my stomach. A little help?"

In a heartbeat, he's on top of me. Undoing the buttons so I'm left in only my bra and very unflattering maternity panties. I can't stifle my cringe fast enough.

"You," he says, dropping to his knees next to the bed, "are fucking perfect." His hands smooth over my belly, down my hips, and along my thighs. "I love you, Wren. No matter what size you are."

"You're just saying that to get into my *very* large under-wear," I tease. But there's a kernel of truth—or sadness—in my tone I can't wipe away. No matter how much or how deeply I believe him.

"I'm saying it because it's true. Because I'm in awe of you, sweetheart." His lips skim my belly, then move higher until he closes his teeth over one of my nipples through the cotton bra. The sensation rockets my arousal up to a million, and I writhe on the bed, arching my back—as much as I can being this huge.

He cups my other breast, and as his thumb keeps time with his lips and tongue, I think maybe I could come from this alone.

I'm so needy, I dig my heels into the mattress. "Please, Ry…"

Lifting his head, he gives me a wicked smile. "You want something, little bird?" He slides one hand under me and flicks open the catch on my bra.

My breasts are so very heavy and aching for more. I don't have to answer him. He knows what I need. He *always* knows what I need.

"I will never get enough of you," he says with his lips against my nipple. "I can't believe you didn't run away. That you saw me—the real me—and didn't run."

"I still see you," I manage. If he doesn't take my panties off in the next few seconds, I might implode. "Now help me off with these."

I tug at the cotton, and he obliges, baring me to him.

Then he's between my thighs. His tongue laps at my folds. Slowly at first, then quicker as he finds his rhythm. The sensations…they're so very different than they used to be. But somehow, they're still like coming home in a way I never knew I needed.

He slides one finger inside me, then another, pumping them in and out as he licks, sucks, and bites until I can't remember my own name. Nothing exists but the two of us— and the pleasure building to a peak so quickly, it takes my breath away.

Ryker growls against my clit, and I fly.

I don't know how long it takes me to come down. Two minutes? Five? But when I do, he's holding me close. And he found time to remove his briefs.

A bead of precum glistens at his tip. "Well, don't just lie there, soldier. Take me."

He doesn't move. "You don't...you have to go to the doctor..."

It takes me a full minute to figure out why he's suddenly embarrassed. "Flippin' flapjacks. You think I'm the first pregnant woman who had sex right before going to the doctor? Who came in with...err...?"

"Maybe?"

My eyeroll is worthy of an Academy Award. "Get inside me. Now."

He lays me against the pillows and straddles me—as best he can with my belly in the way—but when he slides home, I don't care that my legs are almost folded in half.

He's gentle—and not—thrusting with a punishing rhythm that would shake the entire bed if he hadn't bolted it to the floor not long after I moved in.

The feel of him inside me, of his dick getting harder with each thrust, is something I'll never tire of. When his eyes start to roll back in his head, I grab his ass and pull him closer.

He shouts my name as he flies apart over me. He doesn't see it. What he looks like when he lets go. How all the darkness he carries with him every other minute of every day simply vanishes when we're connected.

Knowing I can give him this—even briefly—is all I'll ever need. Besides him and our daughter.

CHAPTER EIGHT

Ryker

"You stay by my side the entire time."

I don't like leaving the condo. Not when we're still unsure if there's an actual threat. But Wren's had dizzy spells for two days, and outside of emergencies, her doctor doesn't work on weekends. I don't know shit about babies, but I'm pretty sure our kid isn't going to avoid being born because I'm worried about our safety.

Wren finishes buttoning her dress and smooths her hands over her belly. "The doctor's going to want to examine me. Like...*really* examine me."

"I'm staying in the room. I'm not leaving you alone."

"And what if she wants to induce me? There'll be stuff happening. *Medical* stuff. Stuff you might not want to see."

I stare her down. "Fifty-four bones, little bird. I set every one of them. And half of Dax's. I can handle *medical* stuff." She doesn't understand how worried I am. How strange it is that she, Ripper, *and* Zephyr can't find any trace of this guy.

"Fine. You try telling the doctor you won't leave and see

how well that goes over." She shakes her head, but there's love reflected in her gaze. "Can we go now?"

I check my phone, relieved when I see the latest text message. "Yep. West is downstairs waiting for us."

"Oh, my God. Really?"

"Really." I hike her go bag onto my shoulder and rest my other hand at the small of her back. She stays close all the way to the parking garage, where West leans against his vintage powder blue F150 pickup. The former SEAL looks like he doesn't have a care in the world—to anyone who doesn't know him. But his eyes are always moving, scanning the garage all the way out the barred windows to the street. And from the slight bulge under his jacket, he's packing.

"You in labor yet?" he asks.

"No. But I think I'm close," Wren says. "Let's hope close enough."

"Want me to follow or ride with you?"

I finger my key fob. "Take your own wheels. Who knows what's going to happen once we get there. We could be there a while. If so, we'll figure out a plan."

At the word "plan," Wren snorts. "You are *not* going to set up a security rotation around my hospital room."

I cut my gaze to hers. "Watch me."

It's twenty minutes before they show us to a room, have Wren change into a gown, and pee in a cup. Then a haggard-looking nurse straps a monitoring harness to her belly, enters half a dozen numbers into the computer, and leaves us with a quick, "The doctor will be in soon." West is stationed in the hall. I stand at the window, staring down at the parking lot below.

No one followed us—at least no one we could see. The

nurse assured us it would be only her and Wren's doctor in the room. And I'm armed.

Wren wasn't happy when she realized I had a pistol strapped to my ankle, but I'm not taking chances.

"Ry, for fork's sake, sit down."

"Fork's sake? That's a new one." I move to her side and take her hand. "I have to find a way to stop swearing. Maybe Royce can design some sort of electric-shock wearable for me."

Wren shakes her head. "Nope. You'd be dead in less than four hours. We're just going to have to teach Harlow that those words are for home only."

The idea of teaching our kid *anything* is scarier than going back to Hell. "I'll teach her how to fight and protect herself. But if I try to teach her not to swear in public, I'm afraid every other word out of my mouth will be 'fuck.'"

She laughs, and her free hand flies to her belly. "She's kicking again. Hard. We're going to have to swaddle her or she'll bounce right out of the crib."

"Fuck. Something else I don't know how to do." I scrape my fingers over my bald head, feeling the scars from too many boots, knives, and fists. "How the hell are we supposed to do this?"

"Ry." Wren sits up a little straighter on the exam table. "I'm scared too. But our parents did it. So did their parents. And their parents. Back thousands of years. We're going to make mistakes. We're going to be exhausted and we're probably going to fight a little more because of how tired we are, but we can do this. We have family. So much family. And the internet."

I'm about to tell her none of this makes me feel any better when there's a brisk knock at the door, and the doctor pokes her head in. "Ready for me?" she asks.

"Yes. Please, *please* tell me this baby is ready to be born," Wren says.

"Let's find out." Dr. Wright sinks down onto a stool and snaps on a pair of gloves. "A little pressure now." After a minute with her hand between Wren's legs, she hums. "You're only a little over two centimeters. Any contractions?"

"No." The disappointment in Wren's voice hits hard. "But I've been dizzy the past couple of days and I just feel...off."

"Well, this late in pregnancy, most women feel a little out of sorts. But I'm not going to discount a mama's intuition." She strips off her gloves and tosses them in the trash. "You can get dressed. It'll be a few minutes before your blood sugar numbers come back, though. Your last test was normal, but sometimes these things go wonky toward the end."

"Wonky? What's that supposed to mean?" I ask. "Is there something wrong or not?"

Her brown eyes narrow and she stares up at me like she's just realized I'm here. "I have no way of knowing until I get her test results back. But it's probably nothing. Your wife is carrying a tiny human, and sometimes, the body gets overwhelmed the last few days or weeks. If there is something wrong, we'll find it. But we're a bit backed up today, so it might be fifteen or twenty minutes. Try to relax, okay?"

She's out the door before either of us can answer.

"Relax," I mutter. "I'd like to see *her* relax if she were in this situation."

"She has two kids. She's been in this exact situation before. Plus, she's the best ob/gyn in the city." Wren takes my hand and strokes her thumb back and forth across my wrist.

The urge to stalk after the doc and threaten her until she admits Wren to the hospital is so strong, I almost pull away.

"Help me up, big guy. And get my dress? These gowns are itchy and it's freezing in here."

I do as she asks, but only seconds after she finishes doing up the buttons, she sways on her feet.

"Whoa."

"What's wrong?" I wrap my arm around her waist. Her eyes are glassy and she's too pale.

"Dizzy again. And hungry. There was a vending machine by the reception desk. Can you get me a bag of dill pickle chips, a package of Oreos, and a ginger ale?"

"I'm not leaving you. I'll call West."

"Freakin' fishsticks, Ry. We're in a busy medical center. Surrounded by doctors and nurses and security guards. Nothing's going to happen to me here. I have my panic button." She pulls her phone with its stick-on panic button out of her dress pocket and waves it at me. "I'm not leaving this room until the nurse comes in. You'll be able to see the door the whole time. You *and* West."

I can't refuse. Mostly because she's right. There's no threat here we won't see coming from a hundred feet away. Sliding my fingers into her curls, I slant my lips over hers. My tongue begs for entrance, and she yields to me with a little moan. She tastes of mint and home, and my fears melt away while we're connected. But too soon, I have to pull away or I'll take her on the narrow exam bed. And if I do, that's when the nurse will barge right in.

"Pickle chips, Oreos, and ginger ale. I'll be back in five minutes. Maybe less. Sit down and don't get up for *any* reason."

"Fine," she huffs. "But once we're home again, we're having a serious talk about all this Neanderthal horsepucky. It's getting a little ridiculous."

"We'll see about that, Mrs. Neanderthal."

In the hall, I stop at West's side. "The doctor doesn't think there's anything to worry about, but they're running some tests. Wren's hungry. I said I'd find the vending machine."

I don't make it two steps before West catches my arm. "Ry? It's that way." He points in the opposite direction.

"Fuck. I'm a goddamn mess. She's my everything, man. I can't lose her."

"You won't." He walks me all the way to the vending machine but keeps one eye on the door to the examination room. "She's going to be fine, Ry. Besides, we're right across the street from the hospital."

I punch A13 on the machine's keypad and wave my phone over the credit card scanner. The machine beeps, and a package of pickle chips tumbles into the tray. Before I close my fingers around the salty snack, an alarm starts to blare, and a strobe light flashes over the nurse's station.

West and I move in a heartbeat, but as we turn, heavy fire doors slam shut, cutting us off from the exam rooms. And Wren.

"Fuck!" I throw myself against the doors to no avail. Sampson lends his weight too, but they're locked tight.

"Call her," he shouts and sprints back to the nurse's station. "Get these doors open!"

Wren answers on the first ring. "Ry? Is there actually a fire?"

"We don't know. But unless you smell smoke, do *not* leave that room. The fire doors are locked and we can't get to you."

"They'd only do that if there were an actual fire, right?" The fear in her voice slays me, and I'd punch a hole in the wall to get to her if I thought it'd work.

"I don't smell anything, sweetheart. It's got to be a malfunction. But stay put. West and I will be there in five minutes. Maybe less. If we have to crawl through the ventilation ducts, we will."

"I won't go anywhere," she says. "I promise."

"I love you, little bird." I don't want to hang up, but I need both hands to get into the air duct if Sampson can't figure out why the doors won't open on their own. The alarm and flashing lights trigger a headache, but I squeeze my eyes shut and will it away. Or at least into submission where it can't distract me.

"Sit rep," I snap at West.

"The doors aren't supposed to lock. But they're on a closed system. There's nothing the staff can do from here," he says. "Grab one of those chairs so you can give me a boost."

"I'll go."

West stares up at me like I'm off my rocker. "You're three hundred and twenty pounds. Your shoulders are twice as wide as mine, idiot. Do you really think you're going to fit?"

He's right. There's no fucking way.

"Fine. But the minute you get to Wren, you call me. And stay with her until I get these doors open."

"Like I'd do anything else," he says. We drag two chairs close to the doors and climb up on them.

"Sir? What are you doing?" one of the nurses asks. "You can't—"

"My wife is on the other side of those doors. She's nine months pregnant and dizzy. If you think we're going to sit here and wait for some tech with his thumb up his ass to open those doors, you're mistaken."

She must hear the lethality in my tone because she throws her hands up and backs away. I punch one of the lightweight tiles hard enough it cracks in two, then drop the pieces to the floor.

Lacing my fingers together, I form a cup with my hands and brace them on my thigh. "Ready when you are."

"If I find a dead rat up there," West says, "you're paying for all new vaccinations."

"If you find a dead rat up there, there's no fucking way Wren's having the baby in this hospital."

West eyes the crawlspace, then my hands. "On three. One, two…"

Wren

The lights and the alarm have me edging toward a panic attack. Why couldn't Ry have gotten the snacks first? At least then my blood sugar wouldn't be crashing. Assuming that's what this is.

A flutter kick reassures me. "Sorry about this, little one. I don't know how loud it is in there, but you're probably ticked at me. *I'd* be ticked at me."

I jump at the timid knock and almost drop my phone. "Who…who is it?"

"Ms. Kane?" A young man pokes his head into the room. "I'm Bobby, one of Dr. Wright's med techs. She wants you to take a glucose test. Drink this entire cup, and we'll test your blood sugar in fifteen minutes, then again in thirty."

"Oh. Sure. Um…do you know what's going on with the fire alarm?" I take the cup and sniff it. Strawberry this time. The last one was orange and so disgusting, I almost threw up halfway through. I try it, and it's not completely awful.

Bobby rolls his eyes. "We've been having problems for weeks. Yesterday, this happened three times. I'm sure it'll stop in a couple of minutes."

"Good. My husband is freaking out." I choke down half the cup. "They can't make these things taste any better?"

He chuckles, then frowns. "I…uh…forgot to grab the timer at the nurse's station. Be right back."

"I'll be here." A fresh wave of dizziness washes over me. I

stumble over to the window, drop my phone on the visitor chair next to me, and brace my hands on the sill.

"We're stuck behind the fire doors."

The nurse's station is on the *other* side of the fire doors. My knees buckle and hit the floor. My phone. Where's my phone?

Someone hauls me to my feet. "Careful," a man growls. "Ramin said she was not to be harmed."

"Who...?" I turn my head to see who's talking, but my eyes won't focus. Two men. I think. Scrubs. Masks. "Let go... of me..."

"Keep quiet."

I don't want to. I don't want to move, either, but they pull me out of the room and down the hall—away from Ry and the fire doors. Lights flash everywhere.

I'm in trouble. Ry's not here, and someone's taking me. All I can manage is a weak whine. My tongue won't work. There's a ding, and we're moving again.

I get one arm free, but only for a second. One of the men grabs the back of my neck and squeezes hard enough, I whimper.

"Do not fight us, woman. Once we have your husband and his men, we will let you go. You and your baby."

CHAPTER NINE

Ryker

"FUCKING HELL. THERE'S NO ACCESS," West says. His legs dangle over the side of the beam, then he jumps back down onto the chair next to me. His dark blue shirt is covered in dust, and there's a spiderweb in his hair.

Before I can zero in on anyone to threaten, the doors unlock and spring open. We're at Wren's room in ten seconds, but it's fucking empty.

A cup lies upended on a wheeled tray, a bit of pink liquid dripping onto the floor. West spins on his heel and races down the hall. "The elevator just stopped at the garage! I'm taking the stairs!"

He's gone in seconds. I pull the pistol from my ankle holster and sprint for the elevator on the other side of the nurse's station. We're twelve stories up, and while I'm fast, the SEAL is faster.

As soon as the doors slide shut, I dial Ripper. "They took Wren from the goddamn doctor's office. Get Zephyr on the security cameras. We think they're already in the garage."

"Fuck. I'm with Cara. We're headed to the co-working office Dax and Evianna rented for the week to pick them up. I'll call Z and get her started."

He hangs up before I can ask him why Graham isn't with him.

West rounds the corner as I burst into the garage. "They're not here. I checked every car. These were pros. The fire doors stopped us for—at most—seven minutes, and they had time to get Wren out of the room, down to the garage, and into a car. She wouldn't have gone willingly."

How the fuck is he so calm? I can't breathe knowing she's out there alone. Forty weeks pregnant. She must be terrified. I failed her for the second time, and this time...I failed my daughter too.

"Ry." West grabs my arm, his fingers digging into my bicep. "Look at me. Take a breath. In and out. Twice."

I don't have time for this bullshit. But he doesn't let go. "Do it. Or I'll have you flat on your back in five seconds."

"Wren's gone."

"I know. And we'll find her. But only if you focus and don't lose your shit. Go back to the condo. Get Rip and Zephyr on tracking every car that came out of this garage in the past fifteen minutes. I'm staying here. There's got to be someone in this hospital I can *convince* to let me into the security office to get their tapes."

"Tapes? Are you stuck in the eighties?" It's the only thing I can think to say at the moment. Nothing else makes sense. My wife is gone. Taken. And we still don't know why. Or by whom.

If they hurt her, I'll find them and tear them to pieces. I'll make it last weeks. Months. Hell, a full goddamned year.

My phone vibrates in my back pocket. My blood turns to ice at the image on the screen. Wren lies across a bench seat in a van or SUV, her eyes closed.

Unknown: You and your team set off a bomb in Herat, Afghanistan and murdered twenty-three innocents. You will die for your crimes. But your wife will not be harmed as long as you cooperate.

Herat? A bomb? The memories come flooding back like a movie in slow motion. The building was burning when we arrived. We pulled nine people out of the rubble before it collapsed. Six kids, two women, and an old man. Got them medical attention. As far as I knew, they all lived.

I reply, though my fingers shake so much, the words don't come easy.

Ryker: That bomb was courtesy of the Afghan government. We saved people that day. Without us, everyone would have died. Drop Wren off at the nearest hospital. Right fucking now.

Unknown: You lie. We will contact you in one hour. Call no one.

My next message—containing some of the more...inventive things I'd like to do to them—comes back undeliverable. They deactivated the SIM card.

"Get that to Rip. He can clone your phone so we can monitor everything that comes in."

I know that. Everything he's saying...it's what I'd say to him if it were Cam. But it's not Cam. It's Wren. And our daughter. So I don't call him an asshole for telling me things I already know. All I care about is getting Wren back. Safe. If West wants to talk to me like I'm five until that happens, so be it.

"You have comms with you?" I ask.

He pulls a small earbud case from his pocket. "I learned a hell of a long time ago to *never* leave these at home."

"Then go. Get those...'tapes.' I'm counting on you."

West grabs my arm before I can head for my truck. "Ry, this is Wren. No one on this team will rest until she's safe. Every single one of us would die for her."

Ripper

I curl my fingers around the "oh shit" handle in the sedan. Cara takes the corner too quickly, but she never loses control of the car. "Where did you say you learned to drive?"

"I took a defensive driving seminar when I was working at JSOC. I...didn't exactly pass it. I mean, I didn't crash, but apparently you're not supposed to show the instructor how to drift." She shoots me a wicked smile, but the strain in her eyes reminds me what's at stake. Everything.

"You can drift?" The idea that she could play a starring role in a heist movie leaves me both turned on and a little— or a lot—afraid. What else is she keeping from me? "We need to have a talk about all these secrets, sunshine."

"This is the only one. I promise. And it's not a secret. I just rarely get a chance to do this in Seattle. Between the traffic and...well, the laws...I'd never try this on a normal day."

She tightens her hands on the wheel and flips the turn signal.

The small parking garage at the co-working facility is empty. Dax and Evianna rented out the entire office. I'm glad there's no one here. I didn't bring a weapon—beyond my multi-tool—and I'm regretting not grabbing my Glock 19.

Cara pulls into a spot close to the door. I'm about to get out when my phone buzzes. "Shit. It's Zephyr. I have to take this."

"I'll go get Dax and Evianna. Be right back." She gives Charlie—in the backseat—a quick scratch behind the ears. "Stay here, buddy."

"Cara—" I try to tell her not to go, but she's already at the glass doors. She'll be okay. Dax texted me less than five minutes ago and confirmed he and Evianna were alone and safe.

"Zephyr? Have you gotten into the hospital network yet?"

She scoffs. "I'm leaving that to West. He'll have a lot better luck in person. I got into the traffic cameras though. Fifteen cars left the parking garage over a five-minute period around when Wren was taken. I'm sending you the feeds now."

I pull my tablet out of my bag and tap the screen. Playing the first video at three times the speed, I curse under my breath. "Are they all like this? The angles? I can't see inside the vehicles."

"Yep. We need more eyes. How long until you're at a computer?"

"Twenty minutes? We're picking up Dax and Evianna, then heading to Ry's."

"Keep me posted," she says. "If I find anything we can use, I'll let you know."

She ends the call, and I reach back and rub Charlie's head. "Stay here, buddy. And when I get back, you're going to have to sit on the floor. Sorry."

Dax isn't exactly the kind of guy who lets a dog sit on his lap. The man wears dress pants for every occasion. I think I've only seen him in jeans once since he and Ry pulled me out of that well.

Charlie lets out a quiet bark, like he understands what I'm saying, and settles down onto the seat.

There's something in the air when I shut the car door and sweep my gaze around the garage. Something...dark. There's a click, and the scuffing of a shoe on cement, and I freeze.

"Hands in the air, Sergeant Richards. Now."

———

Dax

Rage flares bright hot. I can't *see* the fuckers, but Evianna's quiet whimper is enough for me to turn in their general direction. "Who are you and what do you want?" I growl.

The lights of the co-working space buzz overhead. Cara came in from the garage, and seconds later, two men burst through a side door I didn't even know existed. One of them grabbed Evianna while the other went for Cara.

"Dax Holloway. You killed twenty-three men, women, and children in Herat ten years ago. You and your *friends* will pay for your crimes," a rough, heavily accented voice says.

"I don't know what the fuck you're talking about, asshole. I'm Special Forces. We were all *over* Afghanistan ten years ago. But we *never* killed women or kids. Ever."

"You and your team destroyed an apartment building!" he snarls, and Evianna cries out.

"Don't hurt her!" I take a step, but a third man slams his fist into my gut, and I double over. My cane clatters to the floor. A kick to the back of the knees sends me down after it, and the guy pins my arms behind my back and zip ties my wrists.

Where the hell is Rip?

"Move," the asshole orders. "To the garage."

Cara's first. I can smell her shampoo as she's dragged past me. Then Evianna. Shithead Number Three jerks me to my feet. "Go."

"I can't see, idiot. Or did you fail to notice the cane?"

He mutters something under his breath, grabs my upper arm, and pulls me through the door.

"Fuck. Cara..." Ripper says. "Let them go. They didn't do anything—"

"Neither did Wren," I add. "You shitstains kidnapped a pregnant woman about to give birth."

"We do not wish to hurt any of your women," the first man—who seems to be in charge—says. "We know they are innocent. But you will die for your crimes. Get them into the van."

I can't let them take us anywhere. But when I resist the asshole who tries to drag me away, Cara gasps.

"You son of a bitch," Ripper growls. He's only ten, fifteen feet from me. But that does me no good.

"Rip, what's happening?"

"The big one has a knife to Evianna's throat. The other one has Cara on her knees with his hand...over her mouth." He's terrified and edging toward a panic attack. I have to do *something.*

"We'll go with you. But you let our wives go. Right fucking now."

"Dax, no!" Evianna chokes out.

"You're all that matters, darlin'. You and Cara and Wren. If you're safe..."

The men seem to think for a moment, then the leader— the one holding Evianna—turns toward Rip. "Sergeant Richards, get on your knees. Lace your fingers behind your head, cross your ankles. Forehead to the ground. When you are secured, we will release the women."

Secured. Restrained. Taken.

Rip isn't ready for this. Whatever they have in mind for us. He's barely ready to work for Hidden Agenda on a daily basis. This could break him completely. He hasn't moved, and I can hear Evianna's ragged breathing to my left.

"Rip, do it. That's an order."

I never outranked him, but the words have the desired effect. His hazy shadow sinks down, and the guy holding onto my arm warns me not to move or Evianna will pay the price.

"Cara, I love you, sunshine." Rip chokes back a sob as the zip tie tightens around his wrists, and she screams something too muffled to understand. The tone, however, is lethal. From somewhere behind us, Charlie barks and growls against a backdrop of scratching noises, but he's got to be in a car for how quiet the sounds are.

"Take them," the leader says.

"Wait! Let us say goodbye." I need to know Evianna's okay. That even for a few seconds, she doesn't have a knife to her throat. "Please."

"You have one minute. You try anything, we shoot the women in the kneecaps."

Evianna's arms wind around me. She's shaking. Fuck, I wish I could hold her. Or do anything besides let myself be taken without any guarantee she and Cara will be okay. "Take my glasses, darlin'."

"No—"

"They'll just break 'em." I lower my voice and press my lips to her ear. "I'll need them back when this is over." Her fingers are cold when they brush my cheeks. The fluorescent lights overhead are too bright, and the headache starts almost immediately.

Rip and I are pulled deeper into the garage. It's darker here. A van door slides open. Evianna's heels clicking on the pavement reassures me for all of five seconds before I can't hear them anymore.

Rip is shoved into the vehicle, and the sound he makes is heartbreaking. Despair. Utter hopelessness and terror.

Even now, eight years after losing my sight, I still try to look. To see where he landed. Where I'll land next. I *know* it'll do me no good. I'll never see more than a hazy shadow. But the lifetime I had before is still with me, even though I can barely remember it now.

I think...fuck. Is that Cara crying? They throw me in next to Rip before I can be sure. He's hyperventilating.

"Rip. You will hold it together, soldier."

"Dax..." The agony in his voice breaks me, but I can't let him see it. Not now. Not until we're free and these assholes are six feet under.

"Focus on my voice. You're not back there. You're in Seattle. With me. In a few minutes, they'll let Evianna and Cara go. That's what matters. Right?"

Two of the men climb in with us, and the door slams shut. A hand fists my hair and drags me up to sitting. He smells like vanilla and cinnamon. Sweet and almost cloying. "Did you let them go? Are Evianna and Cara safe?" I demand.

"The women are in the trunk of the car. In a few hours, they will be able to get themselves out."

"Fucker!" I lunge for him, but he slams me against the side wall of the van. "What did you do to them?"

"The same thing I am going to do to you." Something stings my neck. Fuck. A sedative?

"Please," Ripper whispers. "No drugs. Just...kill me now."

"You're okay, Rip. We're...okay." There's no ice flowing through my veins. No instant slowing of the world. But my legs feel heavy. Like they're not mine anymore.

Ripper's choked cries start to fade. The engine rumbles to life, and I struggle to hold my head up. "What'd...you... give us?"

The asshole next to me chuckles. He says something, but I'm too far gone. The words fade into nothingness, along with what little is left of my sight.

CHAPTER TEN

Ryker

I TIGHTEN my grip on my phone until the glass threatens to crack. It's been forty-five minutes since Wren was taken. Forty-five minutes since men put their hands on her.

"I can't reach any of them," Graham says. "But Zephyr says all their phones are pinging from Northwest Cowork. I'm heading down there."

"Not alone you're not. Take Inara with you." No one's heard from Dax and Ripper since I left the medical center. If they're hurt—if they've been taken too, along with Evianna and Cara—the fuckers responsible are going to live for *years* while I carve them into pieces. Starting with their dicks.

"We're not leaving you alone," Inara says. "No way."

"You have to." I scrape my hands over my face. Half of my cheek is numb, nerve damage stealing much of the sensation. "I can't lose anyone else."

Inara takes a step closer and touches my arm. "Ry, you're not thinking clearly. Remember when Coop took Royce?"

Her voice cracks and she clears her throat. "You and West wouldn't let me be alone. No matter how much I tried to push you both away."

I jerk back, ready to snap at her, but the pain in her gray eyes mirrors my own. She's right. But how am I supposed to just wait here without knowing—

The intercom beeps. "Inara? Ryker? Open the door."

Royce. Graham lets him in, and the man limps into the condo with a duffel bag slung over his shoulder. "I came as soon as I could get a car. I grabbed a dozen trans-s-smitters, watch units for monitoring, and the entire contents of our gun safe."

Inara, who came to the condo directly from her office, wraps her arms around her husband. "You're a lifesaver, baby. But I need one more favor."

"Name it." His gaze sweeps around the room, and he frowns. "What don't I know?"

"We can't get in touch with Dax, Evianna, Ripper, or Cara," she says.

"Fuck." Royce gestures to Inara's tablet sitting on the counter. "Can I use this? I'll see if Zephyr can use my help."

"Sure." She starts rummaging through the duffel bag. "I need you to stay here with Ry while Graham and I go to the coworking place Dax and Evianna were using this week."

Graham heads for the door. "I'll meet you in the garage in five. Ry, I'm sending Q up. No one should be alone right now."

Is he worried about Quinton? Or me? It doesn't matter. He's right. Even though this building should be the safest place in the whole goddamn city, they found me. Tracked me down when I've done everything I can to keep myself hidden.

Inara straps her Beretta to her thigh and shoves two spare magazines into her pockets. "We'll be on comms. No one else is going dark."

She and Royce take a silent moment together, foreheads touching, speaking without words. He doesn't tell her to stay safe. He doesn't have to. They're so connected, it's scary.

Five minutes later, Q's sitting on my couch with his cat Clementine curled up next to him. He and Royce have a separate comms channel with Zephyr and Cam, who's in Chicago at a tech conference—now locked in her hotel room with the dresser barring the door.

Pixel slinks over to me and paws at my leg until I pick her up. She knows something's wrong. She hasn't barked once since I came home. With a pitiful little whine, she noses my chin. "I know, pipsqueak," I murmur. "I want her back too. But you know I won't stop until I find her. I promise."

I shouldn't say those words to her. Hell, I shouldn't be so attached to ten pounds of fur and sass. But she's got such a personality, I couldn't help loving her.

"Has anyone called Raelynn and Nash?" Royce asks.

"They're on their way. Raelynn had to get Nash from his studio space. He's working on a new bar top for ZigZag," I say and set Pixel in her bed next to the recliner. She immediately jumps up on the couch and settles down next to Clementine. "She texted five minutes ago. They're fine. And together."

Before long, it's going to be a fucking party here. I wish I could take half an hour to figure out a plan. Or just rage and break everything within reach.

But then my phone rings. Another unknown number. "It's them."

Q tosses me a small black box I plug into my phone. He'll trace the call, but I doubt it'll do any good. Still, we have to try.

"I want to talk to my wife. Right fucking now."

"You do not give the orders. We do."

"I'm not taking orders from anyone who's too much of a coward to give me his name."

"I am Ramin Al Abat. Son of Ebrahim Al Abat. One of the men you killed."

"I didn't kill anyone, asshole. The Afghan government bombed that building. My team and I *saved* people that day. Al Abat? Pretty sure one of the women we saved was your fucking sister, Jamila."

"Jamila lost her leg!" Ramin snaps. "*You* did that. My brothers and I have been searching for you for ten years, McCabe. And now that we have your wife and your friends, you will do whatever we ask."

My friends. Dax and Rip are gone.

"So ask, asshole. My agreement is contingent on you letting me talk to my wife. And her being *unharmed*."

"Fort Worden Battery. Do you know of it?"

"I might have heard of the place."

Royce motions for me to keep them talking, but it's not going to help. These men are good. So good, they have a hell of a lot of help. Including someone who's as good at tech as Wren.

"You will come alone. Arrive at exactly 19:00 hours. If we see any other members of your *team*, or if you are even five minutes late, we will remove Holloway's useless eyes with a spoon and force your wife to watch."

"Be on time, don't bring anyone with me. So original. You do realize that's kidnap and ransom 101, right? So is proof of life. I want to talk to Wren. Now."

The call switches to video. The back of the van is mostly empty. No seats. Dax and Ripper lie on their sides, unconscious, with their hands tied behind their backs. The camera pans to the other side of the vehicle, where Wren sits on the floor. She cradles her belly, and tears stain her cheeks. Her eyes are unfocused, and her head bobs like she's struggling to hold it up. "Ry...?" she whispers. "Don't...come..."

"The hell I won't, sweetheart. What did they give you? Are you okay?"

"Dunno." Her eyes flutter closed. "Back hurts. Don't want to be...here."

The van hits a bump, and she whimpers, tightening her arms around her stomach.

"Wren, listen to me. I'm coming. You're going to be fine. You and the baby. I...I'd do anything for you, little bird."

I want to promise her. But I can't, and she knows it. She's sobbing now, and when she turns away from the phone and curls onto her side, I see red.

"I give myself up, and you take her to the nearest hospital."

"Of course. I am not a monster. Unlike you," he says, flipping the camera around. He's a good looking guy. Full head of black hair, neatly trimmed beard, but yellow, crooked teeth. I'm going to pull them all out. One by one. With a rusty pair of pliers. Then make him swallow them.

"I want your word."

"You have it. As soon as you are secured next to your men, my brother Hadi will take your wife to the nearest hospital. We will do for her what you did not do for all those who died that day."

The screen goes dark, and I throw the phone across the room. It hits Pixel's dog bed and bounces. Before I can stalk over to pick it up, it rings again. Ford's name flashes across the screen.

"Pritchard's trying to get a list of the victims from that apartment building collapse," he says before I can get a word out. "If he can, we might be able to identify these assholes. Our plane lands in four hours—"

"Don't," I snap. "We know who they are now. But that won't help. They have Dax and Rip. They want me—all three of us—to die. They're taking Wren, Dax, and Rip to Fort Worden. It's an abandoned military installation outside of Port Angeles. You won't make it in time, and two more people isn't going to make a goddamn difference."

"We *will* make it in time because Austin just happened to be in Boston. He also pulled a fucking miracle out of his ass and got us the fastest plane on the east coast. And you're an idiot if you think there are only two of us on this plane," Ford says. "This is Wren. And Dax. And Rip. And *you*. Hell, it wouldn't matter if it were any of your people, asshole. Or any of ours. We're not 'two more people,' we're seven. Trevor, Ella, Clive, Ronan, Vasquez, me, and Austin. It'll be nine by the time we get there. Griff is on his way from San Diego, and Connor lands in ninety minutes. He was in Denver on a quick overnight."

I stagger back until I hit the recliner, then sink down when my legs won't hold me. Everyone. All of Second Sight. All of Austin's group—whatever the hell he's calling it. Everyone.

"Like you remind people on the regular, Ryker, we're family. You've done the same shit for every single one of us over the years, and even after that baby is born, I'll bet money you'll still risk your life for any of us. Hell, I expect to see you running workouts with the kid strapped to your chest in under six months. She'll be able to make it up the climbing wall before she says her first word."

The image of our daughter climbing up the wall, her red curls bouncing, a big grin on her face, hits me so hard, I can't breathe. I press my fist to my chest, wondering how I can see her so clearly when she hasn't even been born yet.

"Ford?" Royce takes the phone from my hand. "Ry's...in shock. Not quite s-sure what t-to do about it, but if he doesn't snap out of it in the next t-two minutes, I'll whack him over the head with one of the couch cushions."

"Asshole," I grit out. "I'm right here."

"That's better." Royce drops the phone in my lap and returns to the tablet.

Wren's laptop is on the coffee table in front of me, open, with the screen locked. Will she ever get a chance to use it again? Or will I be staring at it for the rest of my life, convinced I didn't do enough to keep her safe?

"Just...get here," I manage. "I don't know what the plan is. West is still at the medical center. But..."

"Someone will let me know. Good enough for me. We've got your back, Ryker. All of us."

All of us.

<hr>

Inara

A pair of *No Parking* signs bar the entrance to the garage.

"Well, that's not suspicious at all," Graham says as I pull into a loading zone.

"There's an SPU placard under the seat. Grab it and slap it on the dashboard. It'll stop us from getting towed." I shut off the engine and glance around. "This is Seattle in the middle of the day. How are there so few people here?"

"I saw a couple of detour signs a couple of blocks back." He checks his Glock 19 and pulls his black cap lower over his eyes. "There's only one entrance to the garage. We going in together?"

"No one goes *anywhere* alone until this shit is done. Stay in sight."

"Gotcha. I'm on your six like glue."

The kid—he's hardly a kid, though I have at least six years on him—waits for me to approach the *No Parking* sign. It's an official Department of Transportation unit, but there's no notice of any permits or work being done. The garage is well lit, except for one dark corner across from the interior door.

Graham pulls out his flashlight and sweeps the beam across the space. "Fuck. That's Cara's car."

"Clear the area first. Don't get sloppy." We part, Graham going left while I take the right side of the structure. It's completely empty. No other cars, but... "You hear that?"

"Charlie." We draw down on the sedan. The dog barks twice, then whines, then barks again. It's like a signal on repeat. "It's coming from the trunk," Graham says.

If they hurt the dog...

Graham pulls out his multi-tool. "Cover me."

Widening my stance, I take aim at the center of the trunk. The lid pops open and—oh my God. Charlie's pressed against an unconscious Cara, nosing her cheek and whining. Next to them, Evianna moans softly.

"Charlie, out," Graham says. The dog scrambles from the trunk, but he whines when he lands on the concrete and holds up his left paw. There isn't room for both of us to get to Evianna and Cara, so I drop to one knee and take a close look at his foot. One of his toenails is gone, and a bit of blood oozes from his paw pad. He drops a piece of upholstery into my hand.

"You clawed through the back seat to get to them, didn't you?" I ask. He looks around, whines again, and stares back at the car.

"Evianna? Can you stand?" Graham helps her sit up, and she leans against him.

"Maybe..." Her voice is weak. Slurred. "They took Dax. And Ripper. There were...three of them. Or...four. A van..."

She stumbles when she gets out of the trunk, and I let her lean against me. "What did they give you?"

"Dunno. Needle." Her lips flatten, and she pales. "I'm going to be sick."

I get her over to a trash can, and as she heaves, Graham tries to wake Cara up. But while her eyes are open and blinking, it's like she doesn't have any idea what Graham's saying or what she's supposed to do about it.

"Can you carry her? We need to get back to Ry's. Now. We'll call Doc Reynolds when we get there."

"I'm right behind you," the kid says, and hauls Cara up in a fireman's carry.

I wrap Evianna's arm around my shoulders and support some of her weight. Charlie presses himself to her other side, like this is the most important job he's ever had. When this is all over, he's never going to eat anything but steak ever again.

Ryker

Evianna and Cara huddle together on the couch. Charlie lies across their legs like a security blanket. Cara has a damp washcloth draped over her forehead, and Evianna rubs the back of her neck.

"It was like I *knew* something was wrong, but I couldn't do anything about it. I didn't care, either. I think. Everything's fuzzy."

"Doc?" I ask.

Joey clears her throat over the phone speaker. "It was probably a benzodiazepine. Like Valium, but stronger. They're used in dentistry a lot. Minor surgeries too. Ones that cause pain but don't need the patient to be completely out."

"Do we need to get them to the hospital?" I wouldn't let Inara call Doc Reynolds. He got too close when Raelynn almost died. I don't want him here. Not unless there's no other choice.

"No," Joey says. "They're not dangerous—unless you have

an allergy to them. And if that were the case, you'd already know. Just make sure they drink a lot of water and don't leave them alone for the rest of the day."

"The rest...of the day?" Inara asks.

"Yes. Benzos tend to stick around in the bloodstream for a while. Evianna and Cara might seem fine now, but tomorrow, they probably won't remember much of anything from the rest of today."

Shit. How could we have let this happen?

"It was so fast. Cara came in from the garage, and then there were three men with guns in the room with us. If I'd been closer to Dax...maybe he could have done something. But—"

"They knew what they were doing," West says. "They cut the power to the security camera before Ripper got out of the car. Though, even if they hadn't, I doubt we would have gotten anything useful off of it. Another gray van, tinted windows, no clear view of their faces..."

"Doesn't matter. We know who they are now," I say. "Ramin and Hadi Al Aman, Jalal Muhammad, and Mashaal Farrir. Along with at least a couple hired guns. Locals, most likely. Fort Worden is in the middle of fucking nowhere." I lift a picture of Puget Sound off the wall and grab the remote for the large monitor hidden behind it. A map appears on screen. "Only one road in and out. They'll have it watched. Drones, cameras...patrols. Who knows?"

West clears his throat. "I've got a plan. But no one's going to like it."

Inara chokes out a laugh. "No one *ever* likes your plans, frogman. But we follow them because they work. Every time. So tell us what to do."

West holds out his hand, and I pass him the remote. "The Battery is full of old tunnels, bunkers, and passageways. We won't know where Dax, Rip, or Wren are until Ry gets in there with them. But it doesn't matter. Huddle up, and I'll tell you why."

CHAPTER ELEVEN

Wren

I JERK AWAKE, my head bouncing and hitting the hard floor of the van. Another pothole. I think. Wherever we're going, the road is full of them.

Fort...something...? Everything's fuzzy. Like my ears are full of cotton. My brain too. Strange scents surround me. Sweet. Sweaty. Someone puked.

My heart races. Was it me? They gave me something. Koyla. Koyla's dead. Ry killed him. I'm not back there. Not chained to that pipe. Not high.

I wheeze, the panic so strong, I'm about to lose myself to it.

"Wren."

The deep voice shocks me enough to open my eyes. Dax. He's on his side across from me.

"Breathe," he says. His voice is thick, and he groans as he stretches his legs.

A dark shadow moves between us. "Quiet!" one of the

men who took me shouts. He punctuates his order with a swift kick to Dax's torso.

"She's...panicking...asshole," he manages. "What...do you think...is gonna happen if she's not okay when Ryker... shows up?"

I dig my fingers into my palms until I can't stand the pain any longer. It helps. Enough for me to take an unsteady breath. Nausea rolls through me. Pressure tightens a band around my stomach, building from just under my ribs and moving down like a wave.

No. Not here. Not like this. I try to feel between my legs, but my limbs are so heavy. My water hasn't broken. Not yet. At least...I don't think so.

The walls pulse all around me like some sort of demented fun house. Darkness creeps along the edges of my vision, and my head tingles.

The disgusting strawberry drink threatens to come back up. I should have known what was happening. Should have told the nurse to leave until Ry figured out how to open that fire door.

They still would have taken you.

But...I could have screamed. Maybe someone would have heard me. I don't remember much after they grabbed me. Snatches. The elevator doors closing. A blanket. Then a whiff of fresh air before I landed on this hard floor.

I have to do something. Find a way to get myself out of this mess. Dax and Rip too.

"I'm going to be sick," I moan and try to curl into a ball. "I need water..."

The guy who kicked Dax mutters something under his breath, but he unzips a large duffel bag and retrieves a bottle, then tosses it at my feet.

I could reach it, but if they think I'm more out of it than I am, maybe they'll let down their guard? "Help me..."

"You are an idiot, Mashaal," the man in the front passenger seat says sharply. "And we are not monsters. Sit down."

Mashaal sinks down at the back of the van, while the other man makes his way over to me. "I am sorry for this, Mrs. McCabe. We do not wish to hurt you." He helps me sit up, twists the cap off the bottle, and holds it to my lips.

It's warm, but it helps banish the sickly sweet remnants of strawberry and drugs. "Who are you?" I whisper when he reseals the bottle and sets it next to me.

"My name is Ramin. My brother, Jalal, is driving. Mashaal is my cousin, and his brother Hadi is following us. We have been looking for your husband for many years."

"Why?"

Ramin settles down, sitting cross-legged with his hands on his knees. "Because ten years ago, the United States Special Forces bombed the apartment building we lived in." He pulls up the sleeve of his dark brown tunic to reveal terrible burn scars all the way up to his elbow. "Many people died that day. Others...suffered."

"We didn't bomb the building," Dax says, and Mashaal springs up and punches him in the face. His head snaps back and hits the wall of the van.

"Please..." I cradle my belly, hoping my daughter will kick and let me know whatever they gave me isn't hurting her. "Don't do this. If you let us go—"

His expression hardens. That was the wrong thing to say. My legs shake as I pull them up to try to protect my baby, but he doesn't strike me. "You, we will release. But McCabe and those two," he cuts his gaze to Dax and Ripper, "will die."

Tears spill over onto my cheeks. He can't let me go. "I know your names. And your faces. You're going to kill me too, aren't you?"

He's almost tender as he reaches out and lays his palm on

my belly. "No. I give you my word. When McCabe, Holloway, and Richards are dead, we will leave this world knowing we have brought honor to our families. It does not matter that you can identify us. Because we will be in Jannah."

I want to squirm away from his touch. "What's...Jannah?"

"Heaven."

I DON'T KNOW how long we've been driving. But at least ten or fifteen minutes have passed since Raman gave me water. Dax hasn't moved since Mashaal punched him. Ripper is staring straight ahead, his eyes glassy, and shaking. I wish I could help him. But another cramp—this one much stronger—rolls through me, and I drop my head to my knees.

Is this labor? I wish I knew for sure. Though, would Ramin be able to tell that it's not? If I act like I'm about to give birth, would he take me to the hospital now? Or would he even care?

I don't trust him to actually let me go. If I cause trouble, he could hurt me. Or kill me before Ryker can get to wherever the heck we're going. I need to see him one more time. To tell him I love him. To tell him this isn't his fault. If he can't find a way to rescue me—Dax and Rip too—he'll never forgive himself.

Reaching for the bottle of water, I try to remember what the books told me. Early labor can last for hours. Even a day. I was only two centimeters earlier. I can't be much more than that now. Right?

"How much longer?" I ask, and let my head fall back against the side of the van. Let them think I'm not doing very well. I need them to underestimate me if I have any hope of getting out of this. "Gonna need...to pee soon."

Ramin turns and frowns at me. "Forty-five minutes. We cannot stop. I am sorry."

Well, that sucks. But he leans closer to the driver and tells him to go faster, then starts texting someone. What I wouldn't give to get my hands on his phone.

"Wherever...we're going..." I say, purposely slurring my words and closing my eyes, "there better be a bathroom. You...have no idea...how often...pregnant women need to pee."

BY THE TIME the van coasts to a stop, everything hurts. My contractions—and I'm sure they *are* contractions now—are fifteen minutes apart. How much longer do I have? Four hours? Less?

I lied earlier about needing to pee, but when Ramin lifts me to my feet, I regret drinking that entire bottle of water.

"Please let me go," I whimper as the side door to the van slides open and a beam of sunlight slices into the dim interior. "You don't need me anymore."

"Your husband will not give himself up if we do not show him proof of life," Ramin says. He's almost apologetic. "Mashaal, if Holloway or Richards move, shoot them in the kneecaps. Hadi, Malik, and Wadid will help you secure them in the bunker. I need Jalal to help me with Mrs. McCabe."

"Don't separate us!" I cry. "Please!"

We haven't been allowed to talk. I'm not sure Ripper's even lucid. But they're my only connection to *anything* right now, and I'm terrified of what's going to happen to them and to me.

"You do not want to see what comes next," Ramin says softly. "I swear to you, as long as your husband gives himself up to us, by the end of today, this will all be nothing but an unpleasant memory."

Jalal takes one arm, Ramin the other, and they muscle me out of the van.

"Dax! Ripper!"

"Tell Evianna..." Dax says, but then Mashaal whips him across the face with his pistol.

Panic tightens in my chest. I can't see them anymore. Or hear them. Only the wind whipping around us. This used to be a parking lot, but huge clumps of grass and weeds are growing up through cracks in the asphalt.

My legs are wobbly, but Ramin and Jalal keep me upright as we make our way through rusty metal gates. Within a minute, we're surrounded by cracked, mossy concrete, the massive structures in eerie disrepair.

Down a long set of stairs, they pause outside a narrow opening. "Take her to the toilet, then lock her in the second bunker," Ramin says. "Bring her food, water, and a blanket. She should not be made to suffer." He turns to me. "I am sorry for this. But you will be home soon. Do not worry."

Jalal pushes me into the shadowy passageway before I can respond. It's so narrow, he can't stay at my side, but instead makes me shuffle ahead of him. It's a maze. A right turn, then a left, then another left. The overhead lights flicker and buzz, and though I've never believed in ghosts, I'm sure this place is haunted.

"How much farther?" I ask, slumping against the wall when I can't hold myself up any longer.

"Not far," he says softly. He's smaller than Ramin. Weaker.

If I have any hope of escaping, I have to do it before we get to the bunker. Before I'm "locked up" somewhere no one will ever find me.

I twist around, ball my hand into a fist, and slam it into Jalal's balls. He goes down with a high-pitched shriek. I take off down the passageway as quickly as I can—which isn't very fast given my size and how badly I have to pee. But two more turns, and I see daylight. I want to cry when I burst out of the tiny space. To my left, bunker after bunker after bunker. All with heavy metal doors. To my right, a massive concrete theater at least two hundred feet across. The only way out looks to be a rusty ladder at the far end. I have to try.

But before I make it more than ten steps, another contraction, this one so much more painful than any of the others, sends me to my knees with a wail.

Jalal grabs my arm and yanks me up, rage in his brown eyes. "Did you think you could get away?" he snaps. "There is nowhere to go." He twists my arm behind my back, and I cry out. "I did not wish to hurt you, but you left me no choice."

Panic holds my chest in a vise. I start to hyperventilate as he forces me into the bunker. It's cold in here. A long metal conduit with two lights runs across the space, but only one of them works.

Liquid drips down my legs and soaks into my socks. Oh, God. My water just broke. Darkness creeps along the fringes of my vision.

"Help...me," I wheeze.

"No." He releases my arm, and seconds later, slams the door and locks me in.

I sink down to my hands and knees, rocking back and forth and sobbing. I'm alone. In active labor. With no way out.

CHAPTER TWELVE

Ripper

I DON'T KNOW what's real anymore. Stale air wafts over my cheeks. I can't feel my hands. A concrete floor swims in and out of focus. Along with my bare feet.

Water sloshes between my toes. Where are my shoes? Fuck. I'm tied to a chair with a plastic tub under my feet. My t-shirt is ripped down the middle, exposing my torso. That can only mean one thing.

"Fuck. You!" Dax shouts from my left. His long, low scream is followed quickly by the smell of burnt flesh. My stomach roils, and I barely manage to turn my head before I lose the little I ate this morning.

The battery cables sizzle as a tall, dark-haired man snaps the leads against one another. Dax is bound much like I am. Blood drips from his split lip. His white dress shirt is spattered with it. He's still twitching from the shock, and a burned patch of skin darkens his side.

"We have two hours," the man growls and advances on him again. "Ramin says we can make you suffer."

"Stop," I groan. "We didn't set off that bomb."

"Rip...shut up." Dax spits at the guy as he heads for me. "That's a goddamn order."

Another man with a short length of pipe steps out of the shadows. The hit to my gut doesn't surprise me. I've taken enough of them. But the pain flares bright hot, and tears spring to my eyes.

"Tell us why you targeted our families," the first guy growls.

"Are you deaf, asswipe?" I glare up at the guy holding the cables. "We didn't."

The leads crackle, and I steel myself for the shock. But you can't prepare yourself for electrocution. Fists. Knives. Even fire. Those, I can survive. But this...

Every muscle seizes. The zip ties dig into my wrists and ankles as my body flails helplessly.

"Leave him alone," Dax grunts. "He doesn't know a damn thing about the mission. That was *my* job."

Whatever they gave me—us—is still making my head spin. I can't focus worth shit. Can't catch my breath either.

Dax continues to taunt them, drawing their focus away from me.

I can't let myself fall apart. When they took us, I shut down. All I could think about was Faruk. Losing myself to the drugs. The scorpions. The beatings.

But I'm not back there. I'm still in the United States. No more than a couple of hours from Seattle. Cara and Evianna...they're not here. I hope to all that's holy these assholes weren't lying when they said the women would be okay.

"Tickles," Dax says with a lopsided smile after another round with the cables. "You can do...better."

A punch catches him in the temple. His eyes roll back, and his head lolls onto his chest. Fuck. He's out. Too many hits. Traumatic brain injuries. All three of us. Dax has migraines. I get dizzy for no reason. Ry...he doesn't admit to anything, but I know he's in pain. Every day.

"If you want to save your friend another round, you will tell us why you set off that bomb," the guy with the pipe says.

"If you want to save yourself from dying with your balls shoved down your throat, you'll let us go. Because when Ryker McCabe gets his hands on you, he'll carve a new pretty picture into your flesh every hour on the hour until there isn't a single square inch of skin left. Starting with your dick."

The pipe lands across my shoulders this time. I can live with that. I've had worse. Hell, *anything* they do to me, I've had worse.

"You are not that smart, are you Sergeant Richards?"

"Actually, I'm a goddamn genius."

The next hit is aimed directly at my collarbone. One of the most painful bones to break. Hardest to heal too. But I twist my body at the right time, and he clips my upper arm instead.

"I can do this all day. Look. I'm not even breaking a sweat. You took Wren. If you think he's going to let you live, you're fucking idiots."

I shouldn't keep baiting these assholes. It won't end well for me. But if they're busy with us, they're not hurting Wren. Or going after Ry before he's ready. He needs time for West to figure out a plan.

Electricity shoots through me again, so much worse than the last time. Fuck. The leads are only a couple of inches from my dick. I flop helplessly until my vision goes white and there's only a dull roar in my ears. Will I come back from this? Or is it finally the end?

Wren

I pound on the heavy metal doors, hoping someone will hear me. "Eight thousand thirty-one, Eight thousand thirty-two, Eight thousand—shimmyshakes!"

I should be in the hospital. With meds. My birth plan. My *husband.*

Instead, I double over in this big concrete room and focus on one of the leaves on the floor as I force myself to breathe in short pants.

Jalal never came back with water or food. Or bothered to escort me to any sort of bathroom. Squatting to pee in a corner while in labor isn't an experience I ever want to have again.

There's nothing in this bunker but leaves and twigs. And two cameras mounted too high for me to reach. Their red lights have been mocking me for over an hour. I know, because all I've been doing is pacing and counting.

Twelve minutes apart. Eleven. Ten. Now just over eight. If they keep progressing like this, I'll need to push in...two or three hours, tops.

The pain starts to fade, and I stagger over to the wall so I can sink down. My legs don't want to hold me any longer. I swipe my cheeks with the backs of my hands. The baby squirms inside me. Does she know how close she is to being born? Can she feel how scared I am? I rub slow circles on my belly, unable to stop another round of tears from spilling over. "I love you, Harlow. With everything I am. Your daddy does too. You know that, right? Whatever happens, you are loved."

Whatever happens.

If I have to give birth here—alone—will we even survive? Will I have the chance to hold her? To hear her cry? It's so cold in here. I won't be able to keep her warm.

I stare up at the camera and let all my rage and terror spill over. "Can you hear me, assholes? Are you watching this? You know I'm in labor. If you were telling the truth—that you don't want to hurt me—take me to the hospital."

The red light blinks. Twice. Then turns off completely. I'm alone. Truly and utterly alone. The idea that my kidnappers knew I was in labor and ignored me was heartbreaking, but now, I could die in this bunker—along with my daughter—and no one will ever know.

I curl onto my side and wrap my arms around my belly. "I'm so sorry, baby girl. Mama couldn't protect you."

***

Dax

"Wake up, man." A hand slaps my face lightly, and I force my eyes open. A diffuse light shines from somewhere overhead, casting shadows over me. "Thank fuck," Rip says. "Can you move?"

He helps me sit up, and the world spins around me so fast I topple against him with a groan.

"You're in bad shape. What the hell were you thinking, baiting them like that?"

"Dunno."

That's a lie. I knew *exactly* what I was doing, and though we were trained to never lie to our team, there's no way I can tell Rip the truth.

He's quiet for a moment, then sighs. "Bullshit. You didn't think I could handle it, so you decided to pull a Ryker."

I choke out a laugh, then regret it when my cheek, jaw, and ribs send pain crackling through my body. "Pull a... Ryker? Don't let him hear you say that. We'll never live it down."

"You're assuming we're going to live more than another hour," he says.

Gingerly, I touch my left wrist. The deep welt is sticky with blood. "We might. They untied us, didn't they?"

Rip snorts. "No. That was me. Took for-fucking-ever to break the chair. Even longer to punch through the zip ties with a rusty nail I found on the floor. If we do get out of here, we need to update our tetanus shots."

Fuck. "You did all that?"

"I'm broken, Dax. Not useless."

A tidal wave of guilt crashes over me at the hurt in his tone. "Rip, I'm sorry. I didn't mean—"

"Yeah, you did. And it's my fault. I've been so stuck in my own head since we rescued Hope, I didn't see how worried you all were. I lost my confidence. Not my skills."

"Well, those skills are fucking impressive." I pinch the bridge of my nose. "Any idea what time it is?"

"Sometime around six? One of those assholes was wearing a watch. They left around 5:30."

"Fuck. Ramin told Ry to be here at seven. We've got an hour to find a way out of here or he's going to give himself up."

Rip snorts again. "Ry's not going to give himself up. Not without a plan. I'm sure Sampson's on it. But if we're still stuck in here, we're nothing but two sad sacks of liability."

"I'm not sad. I'm fucking pissed. This was one of my favorite shirts."

"You're blind. You can't see it. How do you even *have* a favorite shirt?"

"It's a Royal Oxford. Evianna gave it to me." I touch my wedding ring. Thank God they didn't take it. "You said you broke the chair? Any planks big enough to do major damage?" I ask.

"Not really. Though yours is still in one piece."

I rest my head against the wall. It's cool, and it helps soothe my headache. "What else do you see?"

"Not much. Two plastic kiddie pools. A couple of dead rats. They took the car battery, cables, and pipe with them. There's a camera over the door. Blinking red light and everything."

I turn, staring at him though I can't see much more than a dark-haired blur. "There's a camera. Watching us. And you broke the chair, busted through four sets of zip ties, and *no one's come* to beat the shit out of us again?"

"Fuck." Ripper gets to his feet and shuffles halfway across the room. He's silent for a full minute. Maybe two. "It's not blinking. It's...communicating. 'Be. Ready.'

"What the hell is that supposed to mean?" I ask.

Rip's bare feet make little sound on the cold concrete floor. But when he grabs the chair and drags it over to me, I push up on to my knees. "Guess we'll find out. Let's see what we can do with this chair."

CHAPTER THIRTEEN

Ryker

THE BLACKHAWK'S blades pick up speed, the *whoop, whoop, whoop* almost comforting. Raelynn adjusts her headset, and next to her, West checks the pockets of his tactical vest. The SEAL has his rituals. We all do. But mine don't bring me any comfort. Not now. Not with Wren out there. Alone. With Dax and Rip gone.

Graham hauls his rucksack over his shoulder and heads for the bird. Inara's already on board. Griff and Connor too. The former FBI agent motions for me to hurry up. I check my watch. Sixty minutes until they expect me to show up. Sixty minutes until I can see Wren. Less than that, because I won't get close to them unless I get proof of life. For all of them.

Ford's plane will land at Boeing Field soon. Once Raelynn drops us three miles from Fort Worden, she'll hightail it back and pick up the rest of the team. If we're lucky as fuck, they'll make it before those assholes kill me.

I climb on board, and Inara passes me a bulky headset

with built-in mic. "We're patched into the comms system," West says. "Griff, your glasses keeping up?"

"Don't worry about me. Second Sight's tech is solid." He flexes his fingers slowly, and it's almost impossible to believe they're not real. Pritchard hooked him up with the most advanced prosthetic in the world. One that allows him to *feel* what he touches. The glasses were a joint project. Royce worked with Dax for a year to perfect them. Speech to text at its best.

"Hold on to your butts," Raelynn says. She flips a couple of switches, and we rise smoothly from the helipad. "Until we get out of the city, keep the chatter to a minimum. We ain't got a legal flight plan here, and I gotta watch for other birds in the air. Also...legit birds."

Great. As if I needed anything else to worry about.

The city falls away in minutes. Despite the size of Seattle, it doesn't take long to leave its borders. Puget Sound spreads out under us, and our comms units beep. Zephyr's voice echoes in my ear.

"We have...a development," she says.

"What happened?" My heart races in my chest, and I ball my hands into fists.

"Check your phones. Sending you some footage now."

On screen, in a large, concrete room, three men work Dax and Ripper over.

"How did you get this?" West asks.

"I found the IMEI numbers—it's like a serial number—for the two burner phones Ramin used to contact you," Zephyr says, "and I played a hunch."

"The point?" I don't have the patience for this. Not when I'm watching my brothers being tortured.

"These guys aren't as smart as they think they are. They bought phones in bulk. The IMEIs are consecutive. I tried ten before I found one that pinged back. It's on, and it's connected to wifi. So...I hacked it."

"Can you see Wren?" I ask.

"Hacking the wifi didn't get me that footage," Zephyr says. "It got me a handful of text messages between Ramin and his cousin, Mashaal, detailing exactly how they're going to kill you. Do you wear a cup, Ryker? Preferably one that *doesn't* conduct electricity?"

"So they're going to torture me. Big fucking deal. You've seen me before, Zephyr. I can take it. How did you get the goddamn footage?"

"Someone spiked me," she says.

Next to me, Griff shakes his head. "Care to repeat that for those of us who don't speak hacker?"

"They tried to shut me down. For a lesser woman, this might have been a problem, but I reversed the spike. Long story short, it's bouncing all over the world, so whoever's behind it is a genius. Better than me. Maybe even as good as Wren. But also...I don't think they're completely on board with Ramin's evil plan."

I'm about to tell her to get to the fucking point when she continues. "Because they're the ones who sent me the footage of Dax and Ripper. Along with a schematic showing all the surveillance measures surrounding the Battery. And one single sentence. 'Everything shuts down at 19:10.'"

On screen, page after page of designs unfold. We expected most of this. Drones. Trip wires. Cameras. They'll see us coming from a mile away. Which is why our drop point is three miles from the gates.

"So you're telling me I need to survive for twenty minutes. Ten minutes until this mystery person shuts down the countermeasures, and ten minutes for the calvary to get to me."

"Assuming this isn't some horrible trick? Yes."

West zooms in on the landscape around the Battery. "It's going to be close. These fuckers are loaded."

"How loaded?" Connor asks.

"Loaded enough, if they don't have five or six other men with him—beyond the ones we know about—I'll eat Raelynn's Stetson."

"Ain't no one eatin' my Stetson," Raelynn snaps. "Those damn things ain't cheap, and it's all broken in."

"I don't care how many men he has with him," I growl. "He has Wren, Dax, and Ripper. He's going to die screaming."

"Oh, that's a given," West says. "I'm more worried how much trouble they're going to give us before they start praying to their God for mercy. How much noise they'll make. And how many people we're going to need to pay off." He holds up his hand before I can tell him it doesn't matter. He knows it doesn't matter. That we'll pay anything. Do anything.

But he's right to be worried. To ask.

For the next twenty minutes, no one says a word. It'd take almost two hours to drive from Seattle to this remote coastal town, but less than thirty minutes by air.

"Ain't no room to set down," Raelynn says when we get close to the drop zone. "Y'all are gonna have to fast rope it."

We'd figured as much. West turns to face the rest of us. "Me, Inara, Graham, Griff, Connor, Ry. In that order. Drop quick and head for cover."

He tugs on a second pair of gloves, these designed for a solid grip on the rope, adjusts his ruck, and stands with his boots balanced on the edge of the deck. With a quick glance at the ground, he closes his eyes, then jumps.

Ten seconds later, Inara takes his place. When I'm the only one left, I squeeze my bulk into the front of the bird and rest my hand on Raelynn's shoulder. "You stay 'in the van.' Got it?"

She meets my gaze, her blue eyes blazing behind her tinted glasses. "I don't say this lightly, Ry. But fuck you. I ain't stayin' in the goddamn van any more than you did for me. I got the all clear this mornin'. So don't get dead before I get back, you hear?"

She still carries the scars from almost dying at the hands of the Chicago mob. And though she'll never admit it, she's haunted by almost losing her guy less than a month ago. Yet she didn't hesitate when West asked if she'd fly us out here. Even called in a few favors to get access to this bird.

I've known Hidden Agenda was a family for years. Ever since West postponed his fucking wedding to fly to Russia to help me save Wren. But knowing and believing are two different things. Somehow, until this moment, I didn't truly believe these men and women would lay down their lives for me. But now...I have no doubt.

"Well, get back quick," I say. Then jump.

IT TAKES us fifteen minutes to hoof it two miles east-northeast. No one speaks. West, Inara, and Graham keep exchanging glances like they're having a whole conversation without me.

We pause at the bottom of a hill and I strip off my ruck. In my ear, Zephyr's voice is calm. "You ready to make the call?"

"You're sure this is going to work?"

"It'll work. Wren might be better at hacking, but I'm the best in the world at deep fakes. Especially with this fancy new software Austin bought me last month. Stare straight ahead. Every ten or fifteen seconds, act like you're checking your rear view mirror. I'll do the rest."

West braces himself against a large pine tree, takes my phone, and calls Ramin. He'll hold the device at the right angle, so I can focus on the call. Zephyr's software will modify the video feed and make it appear like I'm in my truck on the highway. Or at least that's the plan. If those assholes figure out I'm really a mile from the Battery in the middle of the fucking forest, it could be the end of everything.

"McCabe. You are punctual," Ramin says when the call connects.

"Let me talk to my wife. Right fucking now."

"You do not make demands of me, murderer. You do what we say, when we say, and how we say." Behind him, another man—Mashaal, I think—holds an AK-47 like a shield.

"You have my brothers and my pregnant wife, asshole. I'm twenty minutes away. As ordered. And I'm alone." I gesture behind me, and damn. Zephyr is as good as she claims. The video shows the inside of my truck, complete with the carseat we installed a month ago. "You want me to conference in my team? They're still in Seattle—and pissed as hell about it. But if you think I'm going to let you lay a finger on me without knowing Wren's alive and unharmed, you're a fucking idiot."

Ramin starts walking, his brother Jalal falling into step behind him. There's nothing around them but concrete. From the photos we found online, they're somewhere on the second level of the Battery. There are dozens of bunkers down there. A maze of passageways, lookouts, and hidey holes. Wren could be anywhere.

"Open it," the man orders and switches the camera view to reveal a set of metal doors secured with a heavy padlock. Jalal pulls out a set of keys. When the door opens, I bite back a curse.

Wren huddles on the floor, her knees drawn up, and sweat beading on her forehead. She cowers deeper into the corner of the dimly lit space.

"Say something to your husband," Ramin says.

"Ry?" Her voice isn't steady, and she's trembling. "You can't do this."

"You and the baby are all that matters, little bird. Are you okay? Have they hurt you?"

"N-no. But Dax and Ripper...they took them too."

"I know, sweetheart. Evianna and Cara are safe. You'll be safe soon, too. You and the baby. When she's born, tell her how much I...I loved her."

"You need to tell her yourself. I can't...I'm..." She lets out an agonized whine that shatters my control. "No. Not yet. It's too...too soon!" Doubling over, she purses her lips, huffing out breath after breath as tears tumble down her cheeks.

"Wren! Fuck. Are you—?"

"Uh huh," she gasps. "Still...six...minutes apart."

"You fucking piece of shit," I shout. "Get her to the hospital right now! She can't have the baby there!"

Ramin swears sharply. "Jalal! You were supposed to be watching her," he growls. "How long has this been going on?"

"Since she hit me and tried to escape. Two hours."

My rage boils over. It takes everything in me not to swipe the phone from West's hand. Ramin switches the video so his face appears on the screen. He looks almost...sorry. "I did not know, McCabe. I give you my word. My cousin, Hadi, has some medical training. He will stay with her until you arrive. The moment you are secured next to Holloway and Richards, Hadi will take her to the hospital. It is only a twenty-minute drive. She will not be harmed."

I can still hear Wren crying in the background, begging me not to come. "The cameras...they had to know!"

The metal door slams shut. Ramin's expression turns lethal. "Twenty minutes, McCabe. Go through the gates and follow the path to the first gun turret. We will be watching."

The call cuts off, and I sink to my knees. "She's been alone for hours. In labor."

No one says a word. West stares me down, equal parts fire and ice in his blue eyes. The rest of them just look guilty. "You fucking knew?"

"Whoever sent Zephyr the video of Dax and Rip sent a short one of Wren too," West says.

"And you kept it from me?" Pushing to my feet, I advance on him. The SEAL doesn't back down. "You don't get to decide what I do and do not need to know!"

"Yes, Ry. I do. I'm running this op." He shoves me hard enough I take a step back. "Hell, I'm running *every* op for the foreseeable future. You brought me in because you knew what I could do. And how well I could do it. I've planned every fucking mission for three goddamn years, and we've all come home. Every time."

"This is my *wife!*" I grab his arms and shove him back against the tree. "You had no right!"

He lowers his voice, the tone more lethal than I've ever heard. "I did. Because of this. Right here. We're less than a hundred yards from the first camera, and you're shouting loud enough to wake the dead. You want them to believe you're alone? This isn't the way to do it."

I let him go, but I can't find it in me to back away.

"Ry? He's right," Inara says. "You would have been out of your mind the whole flight. We still have to disable as many of their traps as we can *and* find a way to get you out of there before those idiots kill you. Any distraction could kill all of us. *And* Wren."

"*E tu*, kid?" I ask, turning to stare at Graham.

His gaze flicks to the SEAL, then back to me. "You've always been the team's rock, Ry. But this is your wife and baby. We all agreed we needed to get through as much of this op as we could before we told you."

"Can we fight about this later?" This from Griff, who holds a small black box in his good hand. "We only have seventeen minutes to get into position. Just got confirmation the truck is waiting for you."

"McCabe," West says, his hands on his hips, "when everyone's safe, you can tell me to fuck off. Or beat the shit out of me. I don't care. But until this is over, I give the orders. Pick up your ruck and move your ass. We have family to rescue."

He's right. Wren needs me. My daughter needs me. I shoulder the heavy pack and meet his gaze. "On your six, frogman. Lead the way."

CHAPTER FOURTEEN

Ryker

The approach to the battery is a long road filled with potholes. The place has seen better days. Then again, so have I. "Heads up," West says over comms. "Alpha Team is coming up on the laser grid now."

"Who the fuck sets up a laser grid out here?" I mutter as I stride toward the rusty gates. "These fuckers go on a spending spree at Recon-R-Us?"

Graham chuckles. Inappropriate humor was *not* what I was going for.

"Any word from the mystery geek?" Trevor asks. "We're five minutes from the safe zone, but it'd be a hell of a lot easier if we could drop right over the Battery."

"I've tried everything to track them down," Zephyr says. "The phone I hacked into earlier is off, so I've got nothing."

I check my watch. Fuck. It's 18:58, and we're out of time. "I'm heading in. They'll search me. And if they take me underground, even the backup comms unit in my boot won't do me any good. I'm depending on you. All of you. Get to Wren. She's your first priority. Your *only* priority."

I'm almost a mile from my team. My family. About to willingly give up control of everything.

"We'll get her out," West says in my ear. "But then we're coming for you, Dax, and Rip too. So don't do anything stupid like get yourself killed. Keep them talking and stay alive."

"Roger that." I slide my Glock from its holster and dangle it by the barrel. Two steps through the gates, I trip the first laser sight. On purpose since I'm not supposed to know it's there.

"Ramin!" I shout as I approach the abandoned gun turret. The mount is still there, rusty metal bolts half worn away.

"Drop your weapons," a man says through some sort of loudspeaker. "All of them."

The pistol is first. Once I kick it away, I remove my knife from the sheath strapped to my thigh. It hits the concrete with a clatter. "That's it."

"Earbud too. I do not believe for even a minute you left them all in Seattle. But they will be too slow to save you now."

I dig the comms unit out of my ear and toss it behind me.

"On your knees. Ankles crossed. Hands behind your head."

"I'll do anything you want, asshole. After I see my wife. You gave me your word you'd take her to the hospital." I turn in a circle, scanning for any sign of Ramin and his men. Four doors in the structure to my left are all open, but it's too dark beyond them to see anything.

"I will bring you to her. Once you are secured."

Fuck. I don't have a choice. She could be anywhere. In any of the bunkers spread out over a square mile.

I sink down to my knees and lace my fingers together at the back of my neck. Seconds later, footsteps approach. A rough hand grabs my arm and twists it, hard.

The urge to kill him is strong enough my legs twitch, but I let him tighten a zip tie around my wrists.

"Get up," he says. "Slowly."

I can sense him backing away, and once he's out of my reach, I rise and turn to face him.

Jalal is barely five-foot-seven. He points an AK-47 at my head, while Ramin stands in one of the open doorways twenty feet away. "This way, McCabe," Ramin says.

It's been at least five minutes since I walked through the gates. If the mystery hacker doesn't shut down the power soon, West better take matters into his own hands.

Ramin steps out of the shadows long enough for me to duck through the doorway and find two other men with AKs waiting for me. "Follow them. If you make trouble, my brother will shoot you."

"No introductions? Let's see. Up front there is Malik. Then Wadid." Jalal slams the barrel of his rifle into my lower back. "Did I get it wrong?"

"Their names do not matter," Ramin says. "Move. Your wife's contractions are five minutes apart now. I kept my word. Hadi has stayed with her. He will bring her to the hospital after you say your goodbyes."

I could break the zip ties easily. Probably kill two of them in seconds. But then I wouldn't find Wren. So I hunch my shoulders and keep my head bowed as I follow them through a maze of dim passageways, down a long set of crumbling steps, and deep into the center of the structure.

Old lights run along the ceiling, some flickering, others burned out completely. Jalal grabs my arm and shoves me so my back is against the wall next to a set of blast doors. A shiny chain with a heavy padlock runs through the rusty handles.

Ramin pulls out his phone. "Bring McCabe's wife to me."

I count the seconds. Five. Ten. Thirty. It's a full minute before I hear her voice down another passageway.

"Where are you taking me? Where's Ryker?"

"We are almost there," a man says. His voice is gentle, thank God. She has to be terrified.

"Ry!" She rushes over to me and winds her arms around my waist, sobbing. "Please don't do this. I can't lose you. *We* can't lose you."

"And I can't lose you. Or the baby. As soon as you get to the hospital, call West. He'll make sure you're safe."

"No! I don't need West. I need you!" She holds me even tighter, her body shaking against me.

I press a kiss to the top of her head. "You have to listen to me, little bird. Tell our *firefly* I love her. That her whole family loves her. Dax's family, Rip's family, everyone back in Boston too. They *all* love her."

Wren peers up at me, and it takes every ounce of my control not to snap the zip ties and wrap my arms around her. But I think she understands. That our family is here. Firefly has always been our code word. It was the only thing I could think of to reassure her.

Hadi wraps his hand around her arm and glances at his watch. "We must go now. Before it is too late."

"I love you, Wren," I shout as he drags her away from me. She's still sobbing when they disappear into one of the dark passageways.

"No! Too...close," she cries, and the last thing I hear is her wail.

Ramin motions to Jalal, who pulls out a set of keys. "And now, McCabe, it is time to reunite you with the rest of your team. I hope you have thought about your last words. You are about to need them."

Where is that goddamn diversion? Without it, will West and the others be able to get to Wren? Or me?

Ramin turns to Wadid and Malik. "Check the camera. Make sure our guests are...where we left them."

Malik pulls out his phone and taps the screen a few times. "Yes, Ramin. They have not moved since the last time I checked on them."

I crane my neck to catch a glimpse of the feed. Dax and Rip are bound to wooden chairs, ten feet apart, their heads bowed.

Jalal tosses the padlock to the side. The links of the chain clink one by one until the man has it wrapped around his fist, ready to use as a weapon. There are too many goddamned guns. Too many men.

The barrel of a pistol presses to the back of my head. "You will take three steps into the bunker and get on your knees facing your men," Ramin says. "So you can watch them die."

I let my shoulders fall forward. Looking broken isn't hard. Not when the lights are still on and death is close enough to touch.

Jalal pulls on the door. The old hinges protest with a high-pitched scream. My gaze lands on a small pile of broken wood where I expected Rip to be, and I grin until we're all plunged into darkness.

CHAPTER FIFTEEN

Ryker

I PIVOT and sweep my leg out to catch Ramin behind the ankles. He goes down, and a shot pierces the darkness. The muzzle flare gives me a split-second glimpse of Wadid aiming his AK into the bunker.

"Fire from your eight o'clock!" I shout.

Bullets spray the back wall, but I can sense my brothers now. They're already out of the bunker, crouched low. Balling my hands into fists, I snap the zip ties. Pain explodes across my shoulders as the chain wraps itself half around my torso.

I grab it, yanking hard enough Jalal lets out an "oof" as he pitches into me.

Light floods the battery—so much for our advantage—but with a quick twist, Jalal's neck snaps, and he's down.

Ripper tackles Wadid, sending his AK clattering to the ground. Mashaal slams the stock of his rifle to the back of Rip's head. The blow lets Wadid flip him and wrap his hands around Rip's throat.

I grab Mashaal's jacket and throw him against the wall

before advancing on Ramin. The asshole scrambles for his pistol.

"Never...underestimate...the blind man," Dax says, each word punctuating a punch or a kick to the guy currently trying to strangle Ripper.

Ramin's fingers close around the butt of his Glock, but I slam my boot down on his hand. Bones crunch under my sole. "Not today, fucker. You tried to kill my brothers. You took *my wife* and she's in *fucking labor!*"

Dax wraps one arm around Wadid's neck and presses his other hand to the back of the man's head. "This is for touching Evianna and Cara," he says and, with a satisfying crack, severs his spinal cord.

Rip pushes to his feet and rubs his hands together as he advances on Malik. "Remember me? You called me an idiot."

"I am sorry! Very sorry!" Malik cries.

I pry the gun from Ramin's broken fingers. "Rip? You haven't had target practice in a while."

He chuckles, and I toss him the Glock.

"Run, fucker," he says. Malik only makes it three steps before Rip pulls the trigger.

I wrap my fingers around Ramin's neck and lift him far enough off the ground to slam him back down again. All the air leaves his lungs in a *whoosh* and he chokes on his own tongue.

"Count yourself lucky, shitstain. My wife needs me."

His eyes widen a split second before I slam my boot down on his neck. The snap should be more satisfying. But the gunfire in the distance has us all on edge.

Rip passes me the Glock. "Go, Ry. We're right behind you."

I should check on them. Make sure they're okay. But all I can think of is Wren. And our baby.

There's no time to dig the comms unit out of my shoe. Or

retrace all my steps. I studied the layout of this place for an hour and memorized a dozen different exfil routes.

Sprinting for a rusty ladder at the far end of the first passageway, I start to climb. More shots, and Connor shouts something that might be, "Clear!"

The setting sun almost blinds me as I reach the top of the ladder. The steady thump of the Blackhawk gets closer. Graham drags a body by the neck, but startles when he sees me. "Shit. Inara took out the guy with Wren. She's on the way to the helo with West."

"Rip and Dax are behind me. Make sure they're okay!"

I double-time it toward the sound of the helicopter.

"I need...*shit*...I need to push!" Wren cries.

Fuck. She can't have the baby here. There's no doctor. We need more time!

I burst through the gates to find her on the ground, Inara at her back, holding her. West kneels at her side, and Ford holds his phone close to the SEAL's ear. "Joey," he says, "you have to talk West through this."

"Wren!" I fall to my knees next to her, and she starts to sob. Her arms wind around my neck, and she holds on as her entire body shakes. "Sweetheart, you can't have the baby here. We have to get up. The hospital—"

"Not...my choice," she whimpers. "She's coming. Now!"

Joey clears her throat over the speaker. "Um, someone has to check if the baby's crowning. Or...God help me, turn on video and let me see."

West squeezes his eyes shut for a beat, then turns to me. "Ry, tell me you're not going to snap my neck for...uh... touching your wife."

All the blood drains from my face. I can *feel* it. West has more medical training than any of us, but this isn't a broken bone or a bullet wound. It's Wren.

"Have you ever done this before?" I ask.

"No. But that's why we have Joey."

"Hey," she squeaks. "I've never delivered a baby either."

Wren whimpers and wraps her arms around her belly. "Not helping," she manages.

"West, check for the baby's head. Now."

The SEAL lifts Wren's skirt and leans down. "Uh, yeah. That's a head."

I take Inara's place, letting Wren lie against my chest with my legs on either side of her. Raelynn, Ronan, and Vasquez come through the gates at an all-out sprint, and skid to a halt when they see us.

"Well, shee-it," Raelynn says. "You two. Go back and get all the emergency blankets and water you can find. And the med kit."

Ronan and Vasquez double-time it back up the hill as Joey encourages Wren to push.

"One, two, three, four, five," she says. "Now breathe, mama. Until the next contraction, just breathe."

West has both of his hands under Wren's skirt. I don't know how to help her. She's clutching my fingers so hard, my knuckles crack. She's so tiny. And I'm...not. What if the baby...what if she can't get her out?

"West? What's happening?" My voice doesn't sound right. If he doesn't answer, it's bad.

"Head's out. One shoulder too. She's got Wren's hair," he says. "I'm ready when you are, Wren. One more push. Maybe two."

"Uh huh." Wren's so weak. So tired. I press a kiss to the top of her head.

"I'm right here, sweetheart. I've got you."

"Never...doing this...again," she pants. "Oh, shit. Here comes another one!"

Joey counts her down, and by the end, Wren's screaming.

I'm so focused on West's face, I know the moment the baby's out. I've never seen him look so...awed.

"Got her," he says softly. Raelynn crouches next to him and slides a gray blanket under our daughter. Joey walks West through how to cut and tie off the cord, and when he rubs the baby's chest for a moment, she lets out a tiny little wail.

"Is she...?" Wren is so exhausted, she lets her head fall back against my shoulder.

"Meet your daughter," the SEAL says. He lays the baby on Wren's chest, and we stare down at her. All the books, all the articles I read online late at night while Wren slept...they all talked about how intensely you would love your kid only seconds after meeting them for the first time. But I didn't understand until now.

The baby cries until Wren strokes her chin, then she suddenly stops and blinks bright blue eyes up at us.

She's not afraid. Doesn't recoil when I give her one of my fingers to hold. She's so small. Fragile.

"She's perfect," I whisper. "You're perfect, little bird."

We're dirty, exhausted, and bloody. But as the baby stares up at her mother, I sweep my gaze over the men and women standing around us. We're surrounded by family, the sun setting in the distance, and I press a kiss to my wife's cheek. "I love you, Wren."

CHAPTER SIXTEEN

Ryker

Joey talks West through all the stuff that has to be done *after* birth, and halfway through some sort of belly massage torture, Wren begs him to stop so she can hand me the baby.

"You won't hurt her," Wren says. Tears swim in her eyes, and I don't think she *wants* to let Harlow go. But the newborn can sense her distress and wails right along with her. "Support her head and...snuggle her. You have to keep her warm."

In an instant, I'm back at the Fairmont in Boston three years ago. We'd only just met, and Wren was in shock after almost being kidnapped.

"Come here," I say, stretching out on the bed.

"I just m-met you!"

"I'm not asking you to sleep with me, sweetheart. You need to get warm. You see anything else in this room as big as me? Until you can manage to get through a sentence without those teeth clicking like a pair of castanets, you'll...snuggle."

The memory soothes me enough to take our daughter in my arms. Or...arm, since she's so small, my hand dwarfs her head. She quiets almost immediately, as if she can't quite figure out who this big brute holding her is.

"I've got you, baby girl," I whisper. She makes a little noise. Not a sob. More like a sigh. Her face is pinking up, and her fine red hair is lighter than Wren's.

"Ryker?" Joey calls. "Take off your shirt and put her directly against your chest. Skin to skin is best. It'll help her bond with you."

Despite how close I am with this group of men and women I call a family, only West and Inara have ever seen my scars. But if this is what Harlow needs, I don't care.

Except, I can't take off my shirt without letting her go. For a full minute, I try to figure out how I can manage it until Rip steps forward. "For fuck's—fudge's sake," he says. "Someone give me a knife."

Inara hands him her multi-tool, and he kneels next to me, grabs my collar, and slices all the way through the shirt.

Harlow settles as soon as I cradle her to my chest. "Can she see me?" I ask.

"She can see you." Wren reaches over and rests her hand on my thigh. "Just keep her in 'cuddle range.'"

She's not afraid of me.

"Hey there, little one. I'm...your dad." As soon as the words leave my lips, my tears spill over.

WREN LOOKS SO tiny in the hospital bed. Her obstetrician was pissed that we took a helicopter back to Seattle, but after West informed her that one of her med techs had drugged Wren to help Ramin's men kidnap her, the doc backed down. And gave the SEAL Bobby's home address.

Harlow slept the whole flight, but she was pissed as hell when the nurse woke her up to run all the tests they normally run right after birth. Wren wasn't much happier when she had to suffer through another round of painful belly massage.

But now, they're both out. I should let myself rest too. Trev and Ronan are taking the first shift outside the hospital room, with Vasquez and Ella scheduled to relieve them a little after 2:00 a.m.

After a soft knock, West pokes his head into the room. "Got a minute?"

"As long as you don't wake them." I push to my feet with a groan and meet him just inside the door. "They're keeping her overnight. Well, both of them."

Concern darkens his blue eyes. "Just precaution, right?"

"Yeah." I stare at the man who found me hiding under a bush after hiking for miles in the snow, barefoot, to escape Hell. He saved my life. Then helped me save Dax. And he's been saving me on the regular for three fucking years. "Listen, about what I said..."

He doesn't look away, but what I see in his gaze cuts deep. "If you want someone else to take over—"

"Fuck no. I was out of line, West. I'm...sorry. You've been the heart of this team from your first mission. Not because you're the best at what you do—though you are—but because you *see* us. Every one of us. There is no Hidden Agenda without you. Or...there shouldn't be."

If he walks away, I'll tell Inara, Graham, Raelynn, and Wyatt to go with him. Because he'll keep them safe. He'll keep the whole family...safe.

West blows out a slow breath and, for a moment, I think I might see a shimmer in his eyes. "I was really hoping you weren't going to opt for the 'beat the shit out of me' option."

We share a quiet chuckle, and the tension between us falls away. "So...everything...taken care of at the Battery?" I ask.

"We cleaned up the mess. Austin 'convinced' the med tech to turn himself in and he's being booked on kidnapping charges now. He already gave them a full confession. But... that's not why I stopped by. Zephyr called. A message came in right before the power went out at the battery. But it got buried with everything else going on. She didn't see it until she logged back on twenty minutes ago."

"You going to tell me what it said?"

West rubs the back of his neck and shakes his head. "One word. 'Help.'"

"That's it?" I glance back at Wren and the baby. They're still sleeping, and I lean my shoulder against the wall. I'm exhausted, but if this is the person who helped us, who looped the camera feeds so Ramin couldn't see Dax and Rip weren't still tied to those fucking chairs, who shut down the lights and the countermeasures at just the right time...we can't ignore this.

"Yep. She's trying to trace the message, but whoever it is... they've gone dark again." He checks his watch. "I'm heading home for a few hours. If she can find them, I'll handle it."

I don't know what to say to the man. This should be my job. Both because I'm the one who started Hidden Agenda and because I owe the mystery hacker a debt I can never repay. But nothing in this world could get me to leave this room. Not with how close I came to losing them.

"West, if you need—"

"I won't." He shakes his head. "You have more important things to do, Ry. Watch over them. And for fuck's sake, wipe that stupid grin off your face. It's scaring me." He jabs my arm, a rare smile curving his lips, and I think this is what it's like to be truly happy.

EPILOGUE

Saba

It's been almost eighteen hours. Pieces of the laptop litter the floor, but no matter how hard I try, I can't fix the motherboard without tools.

My legs ache, and I dig the heels of my hands into the stumps to try to quell the phantom pain. But all it does is bring tears to my eyes.

I finished the last package of crisps before the sun came up. There might be more, but if so, they're in one of the tall cabinets, and I can't reach them.

The dead man's eyes watch me as I claw my way across the floor to the window. Well, one of them does. The other... bits of it are still under my fingernails. He threw me against the wall when he realized I'd shut off the power to the facility. After he turned it back on, he kicked me so hard, two of my ribs cracked.

In his rage, he knocked over the table with the laptop. The power cord tripped him and gave me the chance to slam the computer against his face over and over again until it shattered into pieces and a shard pierced his neck.

The scent of blood hangs so thick in the air, I keep expecting drops to rain down from the ceiling.

Before the laptop screen went dark, I saw McCabe and his men fight back. They had love on their side, and my mother used to say that hate cannot win in a battle with love. I hope she was right.

I will not survive much longer. In the moments before I shut off the power, I tried to send a message to the hacker working with the Americans. One word. "Help." But with the laptop destroyed, I doubt there was enough to go on to find me. If the message was even delivered.

Abdul-Alim—Ramin's cousin—was supposed to kill me, then himself. I should have let him. I am not looking forward to starving to death. The door is locked from the outside, but even if it weren't, this building's elevator is broken. Abdul-Alim carried me up fifteen flights of stairs when he brought me here. The only other buildings close by are under construction.

The sun is high in the sky. It must be well after noon. A spider skitters across the floor. It doesn't care about me. Does it know I will be dead soon?

A quiet click draws my gaze to the door. Is the building settling? Or maybe there are rats. I hate rats.

I hear it again. Scraping. Metal on metal. I sit up a little straighter.

The door swings open, and a metal canister bounces into the room. I watch it with morbid fascination, convinced I'm hallucinating. Until a bright flash and the loudest sound I have ever heard leave me dazed.

The floor shakes. I try to scramble farther from the door, but there's nowhere else to go. My vision is nothing but two bright spots with vague shadows dancing around the edges.

"Clear!" a man shouts.

Someone grabs my hands and pins them over my head. Pure agony wraps around my torso. I can't catch my breath.

"Can you hear me?" This voice is a woman's. I blink hard to try to clear my vision.

"Y-yes. Please..." I struggle against her hold, but she's so much stronger than I am.

"Did you send the message?" she demands.

"Help." I nod. "It was all...I could do. That...and the schematics. The power."

The woman's face is starting to come into focus now. She's beautiful. Glowing, bronzed skin. Gray eyes. A shock of dark hair peeking out from her black cap. I recognize her from the files Ramin made me compile on McCabe and his team. She's a sniper.

The men behind her...I know them too.

"Who are you?" the older man asks. He's a Navy SEAL.

"Saba. Saba Safi."

"You know who we are?"

I nod. "You are West Sampson. She is Inara Ruzgani. He is Graham Peck. I gave Ramin information on all of you."

"Willingly?" Inara's icy tone terrifies me.

"N-no. They took me from my home in Sukkur. Ramin said..." I swallow my sob. "He said he would have my sister killed if I did not help him. But I could not let McCabe and his men die. I found the report on that bombing in Herat. I have proof it was not the American government. Or...had." I nod at the remnants of the laptop on the floor.

"Fuck," Sampson says. "We can't have our information... out there. You've put us all in a shit ton of danger."

Tears spring to my eyes. "I had no choice. But...Ramin hated computers. He could barely work his mobile phone. Everything I found...is on the hard drive."

Peck drops to one knee and scoops pieces of the broken laptop into a bag. "I'll get this to—"

"Not another word," Inara says. She turns her focus back to me. "Don't move. I have to pat you down."

"I do not have any weapons. Not even a pen."

Sampson gestures to the dead man on the floor. "Did you do that?"

"Yes. He beat me when he saw I turned off the power." I gasp as Inara smooths her hands over my torso. Black spots swim before my eyes. "I think things are...broken."

Sampson takes a quick look around the apartment. "Do you have a wheelchair? Prosthetics? Anything here you care about?"

"I have nothing." It's getting harder to sit up. To breathe. To talk.

"We can get you to a doctor if you come with us—well, fuck. Scratch that," the SEAL says. "You're *definitely* coming with us. Because once the doc is done with you, we're going to have a hell of a lot of questions. But after that, we'll help you get back to your family. Or...anywhere else you want to go."

He taps his ear, then lowers his voice. "Leaving with the HVT. Send Superman and Jimmy to wipe this place down. They can leave the DB."

Inara straightens my headscarf, then turns her back to me. "Arms around my neck. Do your best to hang on and try not to strangle me."

"Wait," I protest. "Can you tell me...are Wren and the baby okay?"

"They're fine," Sampson says. "The whole family is doing just fine."

Wren

"I'm perfectly capable of walking," I say when the elevator doors slide open. "It's all of ten steps." Ry has the carseat in one hand but was about to try to pick me up at the same time. "Just go slow."

I'm sore everywhere. Giving birth isn't easy, but doing it outside, on concrete, after being drugged, kidnapped, and locked in a bunker for hours, dialed the pain up to eleven. I'm bruised, swollen, and sitting down is so much worse than standing up or walking. I can't wait to try out the donut pillow that came so highly recommended on the new mom message boards. And sleep in our bed—even if only for an hour or two, since little miss will need feeding again soon.

"They shouldn't have discharged you this quickly," he mutters.

"Horsepucky. The only thing nice about the hospital was the lactation consultant teaching me how to unhook this flippin' nursing bra *while* holding the baby."

"I would have helped with that."

"Stop it. We are not having sex for *at least* a month. Maybe more. Mama's gotta heal. Then figure out when I can go back on birth control."

Ry finishes entering his passcode and presses his palm to the scanner. "You don't have to," he says. "I'll...uh...take care of it on my end."

"Ryker McCabe!" I stare up at him in awe. "Are you volunteering to get a vasectomy?" I don't know why I'm surprised. I think the man would do anything in the world to keep me safe and happy.

"It's a hell of a lot easier for me," he says, his cheeks turning ruddy. "And you said you hated the side effects."

The condo is so quiet. Pixel is staying with Ripper and Cara tonight so the three of us can have a little alone time without needing to walk or feed her. I miss her though. Maybe they can bring her up later for an hour or two.

Ryker leads me over to the couch and sets the carseat on the coffee table. Harlow is caught between asleep and awake. She blinks up at him and yawns when he unsnaps the harness.

I ease myself down onto the pillow with a sigh. "Whoever invented this thing should be sainted. Or knighted. Or something."

My husband steps back, leaving Harlow in her seat and rubbing his hands together like he's not sure what to do now.

"You won't break her, you know."

He doesn't look convinced. "She's so small."

"She's almost eight pounds! That's not small, soldier."

"She fits in my hands," he says. "What if I hurt her?"

"You won't. For all of your over-the-top protectiveness and muscles, you're one of the gentlest people I've ever met, Ry. When you want to be. Pick up your daughter and hand her to me."

I arch a brow and wait for him to melt. He blows out a breath, then scoops the baby out of the carrier. She coos softly, then lets out a wail. Ry flinches, and his expression shutters.

"She's just hungry. There's nothing wrong." I settle back against the cushions, loosen the ties on the peasant blouse, and unhook the nursing bra. "Come sit."

He hands me the baby like he can't let go of her fast enough, but sits right next to me. I turn so I can rest my back against his chest, and he winds his arms loosely around my belly. Sitting like this, it's like he's feeding her too.

It takes her a minute to latch on, and I hiss. The ladies on the message boards warned me how much the first few days would hurt, but I wasn't prepared. Not by a long shot. Still, once she's happily suckling, I can relax and enjoy this new family the three of us have created. Together.

Ryker

Wren sleeps on her side, her arms curled around the body pillow. In the bassinet next to the bed, Harlow is swaddled up tight.

Eight hours. We've survived our first eight hours alone as a family. Multiple feedings, three diaper changes, and a lot of crying. Wren's. Harlow's. Even mine.

Everyone we know has called or texted today. Asking if we need anything. Offering to bring food. Diapers. But Wren and I needed to be alone.

Tomorrow, we'll have Dax, Evianna, Ripper, and Cara over. They all checked in on us in the hospital and got to hold Harlow, but they didn't stay long. Dax and Rip needed rest. Cara and Evianna needed time with their husbands.

An hour ago, West sent me an update on the hacker. Saba. Wren wants to meet her, but I'm not ready for that yet. The SEAL has her set up in a private rehab facility under a fake name. She's malnourished, and the beating she took left her with three broken ribs, a sprained wrist, and a concussion. Along with severe PTSD from the accident that stole her legs fifteen years ago.

Maybe in a week, we'll know enough to be able to trust her, or know we can't.

Zephyr doesn't *think* any of the information Saba dug up on us made it to the dark web. But West hired extra security guards for the building until we can be sure, Royce is working on new biometric scanners, and we've all changed our access codes.

"Come to bed," Wren mumbles. "If you don't sleep when she does, you're going to be in a world of hurt tomorrow."

"I can't stop looking at her." I sink down on the edge of the mattress. "Or you, little bird."

"I look like death." With a yawn, Wren rubs her eyes. "And my boobs hurt."

I dip my head and brush a kiss to her lips. "You're the most beautiful woman I've ever seen. You always have been, and you always will be."

"Liar." She pulls me down so I'm stretched out next to her. My gray sweatpants don't do a damn thing to contain my need for her, and it's going to be a very long month—or more —before I can have her again. "Calm down there, soldier."

"Can't help it. We're going to be in our eighties and I'll still want you just as much as I did that first night in Russia."

"Promise me one thing," she says as she rolls over so I can slide under the blankets with her. "When we're in our eighties, MREs will be nothing but a very distant memory."

I laugh and settle her closer against me.

"I promise."

<hr>

THANK you for reading *Saving Their Forever*. This book means so very much to me. When I first realized I wanted to write this story, I thought it would be—at most—ten or fifteen thousand words (fifty pages).

But with every paragraph, every scene, every chapter, it became more. Ripper demanded more page time. Dax had things to say. Even Inara said she wanted a scene.

And then I realized that this book might mean more to me than any other book I've ever written. Because these men and women are a part of me. They helped bring me back from a dark place years ago. I hadn't written in eighteen months. West and Cam helped me figure out who I was as an author—and a person. With every book, I learned a little more. I'm still learning, as I think we all do.

So, thank you for reading. Thank you for (hopefully) reviewing. And thank you for loving these characters and these stories as much as I do.

Love,
Patricia

ABOUT THE AUTHOR

Patricia D. Eddy is a USA Today bestselling author who writes romance for the beautifully broken. Fueled by coffee, wine, and *Doctor Who* episodes on repeat, she brings damaged heroes and heroines together to find their happy ever afters in many different worlds. From military to paranormal to BDSM, her characters are unstoppable forces colliding with such heat, sparks always fly.

Patricia makes her home in Seattle with her husband and very spoiled cats, and when she's not writing, she loves working on home improvement projects, especially if they involve power tools.

Her award-winning *Away From Keyboard* series will always be her first love, because that's where she realized the characters in her head were telling their own stories—and she was just writing them down.

facebook.com/patriciadeddyauthor
x.com/patriciadeddy
instagram.com/patriciadeddy
bookbub.com/profile/patricia-d-eddy
tiktok.com/@patriciadeddyauthor

ALSO BY PATRICIA D. EDDY

Away From Keyboard

Dive into a steamy mix of geekery and military prowess with the men and women of Hidden Agenda and Second Sight.

Breaking His Code

In Her Sights

On His Six

Second Sight

By Lethal Force

Fighting For Valor

Finding Their Forevers (a holiday short story)

Call Sign: Redemption

Braving His Past

Protecting His Target

Defending His Hope

Trusting His Instincts

Saving Their Forever (an Away From Keyboard novella)

Guarding His Heart

Gone Rogue (an Away From Keyboard spinoff series)

Rogue Protector

Rogue Officer

Rogue Survivor

Rogue Defender

Rogue Operator

Rogue Mission

Dark PNR

These novellas will take you into the darker side of the paranormal with vampires, witches, angels, demons, and more.

Forever Kept

Immortal Hunter

Wicked Omens

Storm of Sin

Gabriel's Gambit

By the Fates

Check out the COMPLETE By the Fates series if you love dark and steamy tales of witches, devils, and an epic battle between good and evil.

By the Fates, Freed

Destined: A By the Fates Story

By the Fates, Fought

By the Fates, Fulfilled

In Blood

If you love hot Italian vampires and and a human who can hold her own against beings far stronger, then the In Blood series is for you.

Secrets in Blood

Revelations in Blood

Holidays and Heroes

Beauty isn't only skin deep and not all scars heal. Come swoon over sexy vets and the men and women who love them.

Mistletoe and Mochas

Love and Libations

Restrained

Do you like to be tied up? Or read about characters who do? Enjoy a fresh COMPLETE BDSM series that will leave you begging for more.

In His Silks

Christmas Silks

All Tied Up For New Year's

In His Collar